RING OF ROSIN

NANCY GOLDEN

GOLDEN CROSS RANCH LLC

This novel's story and characters are fictitious. Any resemblance to actual persons, living or dead, is purely coincidental.

For information or inquiries, email Nancy Golden at
nancy@goldencrossranch.com

Library of Congress Control Number: 2024912658

Published by Golden Cross Ranch LLC
Carrollton, Texas U.S.A.

Cover Design by Piere d' Arterie
https://99designs.com/profiles/pieredarterie

To our son Joshua and daughter-in-love Naomi, the real-life Rugal and Lissa. I suppose that makes Phil and I the real-life Jackal and Mura LOL.

Just as Rugal has found family not all bound by blood, but by love, Joshua also has found family in the Kliskeys. Ring of Rosin is also dedicated to this precious family who has invited Josh and Naomi into theirs, having chosen love to bind them together.

JUST A QUICK NOTE TO MY READERS

As you journey through life, you will meet many people coming from other places and cultures. They may have grown up in another city, state, or even another country. While interacting with people who are not like you may sound scary, it is one of the best things you can do! You will find that they are not so different after all. In fact, you will find your life much richer, as you share about each other's cultures. It's a lot of fun to see things through the eyes of someone with a different cultural lens, and you will be able to learn from each other. And don't forget to try foods from other cultures—you will have some delicious meals for sure!

Don't get upset if your new friend does something that startles or annoys you. Many cultures have diverse ways of viewing the world, and that can take getting used to. Don't be afraid of people because of their appearance. If your cultures are very different, you probably look strange to them, too! You will miss out on a lot of great experiences and maybe even a lifelong friendship, if you don't try to get to know them.

Communication is very important. We must respect other

cultures, but that doesn't mean giving up our own. Instead, we should be willing to talk when misunderstandings occur (in any relationship), each person opening their hearts and minds to the other and trying to see things from their point of view. By doing this, you can achieve a compromise that honors both sides.

The Characters of Elayas, the Terminology of Elayas, and the Kargolith Tribal Ancestry are at the back of the book.

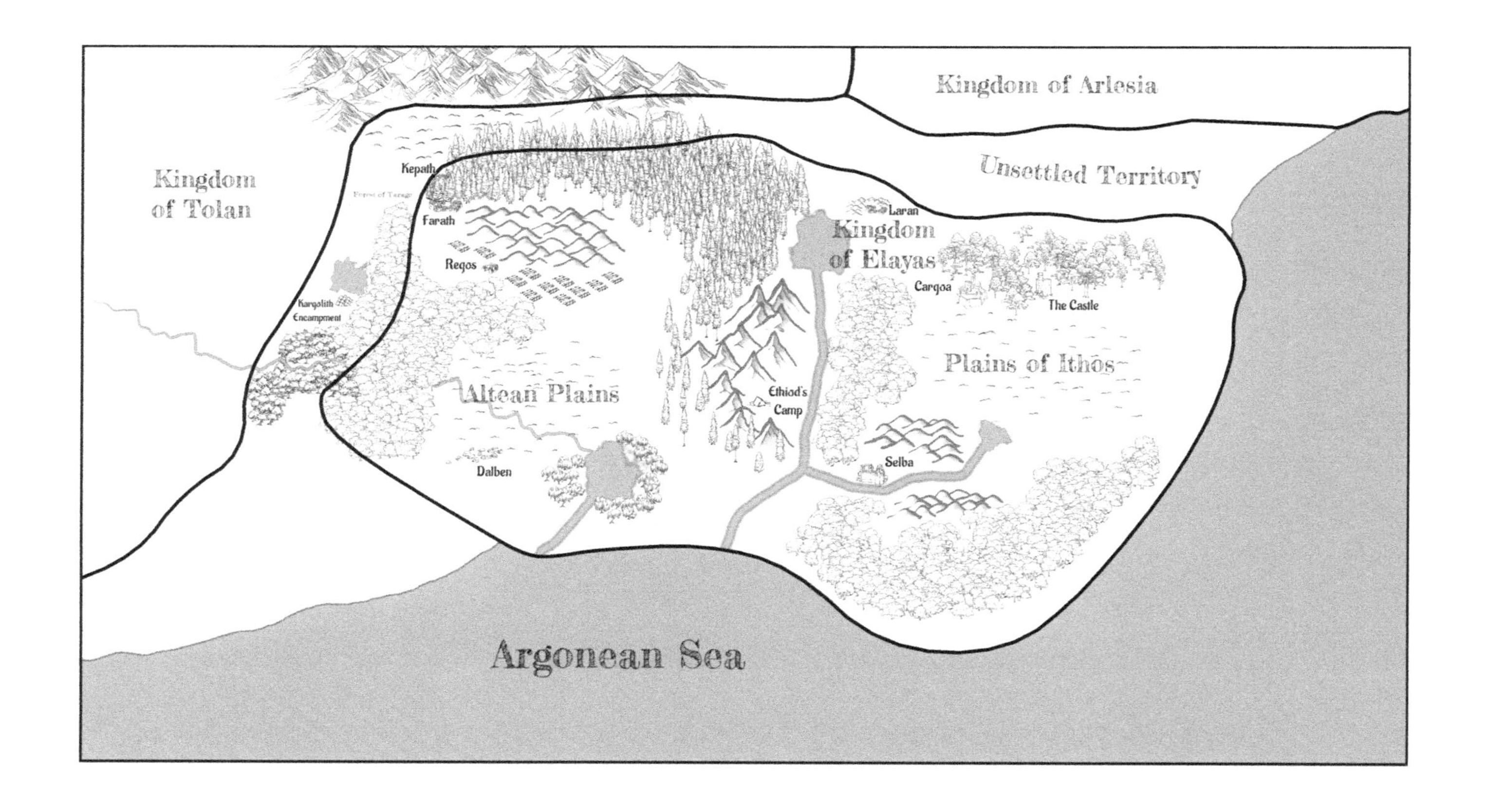
Kingdom of Arlesia
Unsettled Territory
Kingdom of Tolan
Kepath
Farath
Reqos
Kargolith
Encampment
Laran
Kingdom
of Elayas
Cargoa
The Castle
Plains of Ithos
Altean Plains
Ethiod's
Camp
Selba
Dalben
Argonean Sea

CHAPTER ONE

"One should open one's mind to new experiences."
~ Soldar, scholar and member of King Rosin's court

"Sire, the Ring of Rosin is missing!" Melad, the head steward of the castle, rushed into the informal dining room, wringing his hands frantically, his face reddened with distress.

Rugal put his fork down, his lunch forgotten, and stood up, his frame stiffening. He brushed back his tousled brown hair and took a calming breath. "But how could anyone enter the treasury room?"

Melad couldn't form any words in response and, with a heartbroken expression, shrugged his shoulders instead.

"What do you think, Father?" Rugal turned to a wiry man lounging in a chair by the fire. Separated involuntarily when he was born, Rugal had only recently met his birth father and for much of that time knew him only by the name others called him, "Jackal." Their bond had strengthened over their shared experiences, and much to Jackal's delight, Rugal had taken to calling him Father.

Jackal frowned. "I would think it had to be by someone familiar and known in the castle environs, someone who could get access easily." He tilted his head to the side. "I wonder what the motive is behind the theft. The Ring of Rosin is easily recognized so would not be able to be sold."

Rugal's birth mother, Lady Mura, directed her gaze at Melad and asked gently, "How was it discovered missing?"

Melad rubbed his cheek, his hands trembling slightly. He knew he had nothing to fear from the King of Elayas or his family, but he was intensely distraught that the theft had occurred. "I went to retrieve the ring from its customary place. Since King Rugal had worn it recently, I had sent it to the master jeweler to be polished." He sniffed. "I was not here when it was returned by the jeweler's messenger, so I thought I better check the ring and make sure the polish was to the proper standards. When I opened the box, it was gone." Melad reached into his shirt pocket and pulled out a small scroll. "This note was in its place."

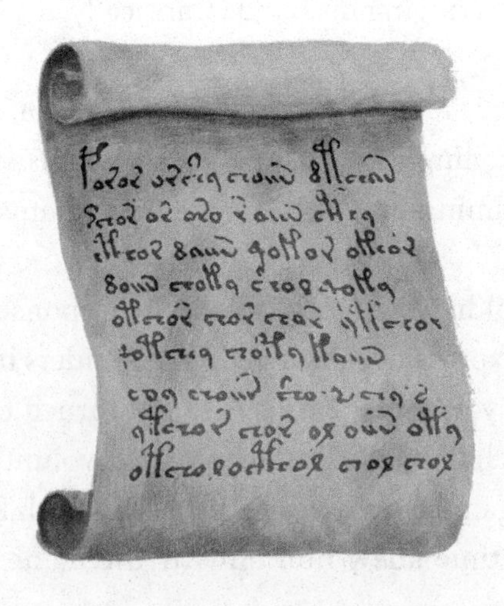

Rugal took the scroll from Melad's outstretched hand and carefully unfurled it. His brow furrowed, and he looked up in puzzlement. The note was written in a foreign script, and he was unable to read it. He handed it to Jackal. "Can you tell where it's from?"

Mura came over and peered over Jackal's shoulder. "I've seen this script before, when my cousin ruled Elayas. Messages from the country of Tolan had this look about it."

"Tolan?" Rugal's eyes narrowed. "Now that is concerning. If the rumors are true, Oldag was born in Tolan. Could it be he has a relative looking to follow in his footsteps and usurp the throne of Elayas?"

A tall, muscular man, the Swordsman sat at the table sipping a mug of ale. He raised his hand, drawing their attention. "Just this morning, we confirmed with a lackey of Oldag's old entourage that he was indeed from Tolan. I think we need to consider every possibility."

Rugal cleared his throat, and all eyes returned to him. "So, we know that the Ring of Rosin is missing. We also have a note we *think* is from Tolan that needs to be deciphered. Is anyone in the kingdom able to read this script?"

"Only one that I know of," Mura replied thoughtfully. "We'll have to ask Soldar to return to the castle. He is quite excited to be in charge of restoring public education." She turned to her son. "Soldar is very familiar with the Kingdom of Tolan. He is also the one who translated messages from King Handerbin of Tolan for King Rosin."

"King Handerbin," Rugal pursed his lips. "He must be getting quite old, if he was king during Rosin's reign."

"That's correct," Mura nodded. "His son, Hamideh, is approaching manhood and will soon be taking the mantle of kingship from his father. We have always had an uneasy truce with Tolan." Her brow furrowed in consternation. "Something perilous must be happening to cause them to break it. We need to get word to Soldar quickly. The longer we wait, the harder it may become to recover the ring. We will also need him to help us navigate how to respond. His knowledge of Tolan is unparalleled."

Mura paused and leaned back in her chair. "Unfortunately, Soldar is in Selba at the moment. He and Ethiod are collaborating with city leaders in opening a Sepharim school in Selba, along with restoring schools for those who do not need to learn about managing *dynamis*. We have to get him here somehow, and fast."

Rugal grinned. "I think I know just how to go about that. I'll ask Treble to fetch Argothal."

THE RUMPLED SCHOLAR pushed his glasses further up his nose, squinting in dismay. "Now Sire, you know I have always made myself available for service, but to ride a dragon? I fear that I should fall..." Soldar's voice trailed off.

Rugal smiled reassuringly. "Don't worry, Soldar. Argothal is very reliable, and I daresay he is safer than a horse. All you need to do is sit between those scales," Rugal pointed, and Argothal turned obligingly, "and hold on. I'll be sitting right in front of you. Argothal will save us several days riding–we would be back at the castle by nightfall." Argothal dipped his wedge-shaped head in agreement, the bluish-green scales shining in the sunlight.

"Well, I suppose I must put aside my fears for the good of the kingdom." Soldar was visibly shaking, and Rugal paused, wondering if perhaps he should find another way to get Soldar to the castle. Just as he was about to suggest seeking alternate transportation, Argothal swung his head around and lowered it to Soldar's height, his yellow eyes gleaming. He warbled softly in encouragement.

Soldar's eyes widened, and he smiled hesitantly. "Ah, maybe it will be okay. One should open one's mind to new experiences after all," he mumbled to himself. Much to the astonishment of Ethiod and Rugal, the older man leapt onto Argothal's extended foreleg, clambering to the place between scales that Rugal had indicated, his sparse brown hair disheveled. He looked down at them with a glowing expression.

"Let's go then, shall we?"

CHAPTER TWO

Your life starts when your manhood journey ends.
~ Tolan Saying

Eyeing his dragon friend wistfully, Rugal gave Argothal a farewell pat. The dragon warbled affectionately in return, before lifting into the air to wing back to his home in the mountains. A flash of blue barreled past them as Rugal's flutebird, Treble, flew skyward to say goodbye to his friend.

Rugal and Soldar made their way up the path and into the castle. Melad stood at the doorway. He had regained his composure from discovering the ring's disappearance and greeted them with a half bow. "Good evening, Sire. It is good to see you again, Soldar. Everyone has gathered in the library, awaiting your arrival."

Rugal nodded his thanks, squeezing Melad's arm cordially as he passed the older man. Rugal and Soldar strode to the library and entered. Jackal, Mura, Lissa, and the Swordsman were gathered around the table in the center of the room. Their conversation came to a standstill, anticipation hanging in the air.

"Soldar, Good to see you," Jackal broke the silence. He moved forward quickly and, putting his hand under his elbow, propelled Soldar toward the table. "Have you eaten?" he asked, trying unsuccessfully to hide his impatience to learn the message contained in the foreign script.

"Yes, yes, I am fine, thank you," Soldar's eyes traveled about, looking for the object that brought him here.

Jackal gestured to a chair, and Soldar slid into it with an expectant expression. Mura stepped forward and handed him the paper that Melad had found. Soldar accepted it, and everyone held their breath as he carefully uncurled the corners. Soldar stared at the words for a long moment and finally looked up at the group crowded around him.

Jackal couldn't stand it anymore and eagerly gestured with both hands. "What does it say?"

Soldar leaned back and blew out a long breath. "More to the point, unfortunately, is what it doesn't say. It is rather cryptic." He looked back down at the note and shoved his glasses back up his nose.

"It is definitely written in the script used in Tolan. It seems to be a rather antiquated version. The language is quite formal."

He looked up at Rugal, frowning. "I have heard of this long ago, when King Rosin still reigned over Elayas. It is the description of an ancient Tolan legend. The words say:

Many, many years ago, a wondrous bird flew into the mountains of Tolan. In its claws, it bore a giant stone, a stone of fire. The bird dropped the stone somewhere in the mountains, where it shat-

tered. The one who finds its fragments shall have power beyond belief.

Rugal's eyebrows drew together. "But that doesn't tell us anything about how to get back the Ring of Rosin. Why would they write that?"

"I'm not sure," Soldar admitted. "The Tolan culture is much different from our own. They have many traditions and legends that are strange to us." His eyes narrowed in thought. "King Handerbin's son Hamideh is Rugal's age. He must be preparing to take his manhood journey soon." He rubbed his chin thoughtfully. "Perhaps this is tied to that journey. Tolan has felt threatened by the people who have made their homes in the unsettled territory that separates them from us. I believe those people, the Kargoliths, will soon be campaigning to become their own kingdom as their numbers grow. Perhaps it is a warning."

"Um, I'm confused," Rugal said, giving a slight shake of his head. "What is the manhood journey Hamideh is taking? And what does that have to do with Tolan securing its borders from outside threats?"

Straightening in his chair, Soldar elaborated, "King Handerbin has been Tolan's sovereign for the last forty years. If his son is to ascend the throne, he must have completed his manhood journey, a custom of theirs that carries the weight of law." He paused and stretched. "A youth must leave his home when he comes of age and embark upon a journey. During the journey, he will have a task assigned to him. The task must be successfully completed in order for him to be recognized as a man in Tolan society."

Lissa moved to stand beside her betrothed, a soft red dress draping her tall, slim figure, her light brown hair put up in a convenient braid that added to her regal appearance. She gazed at Soldar, her eyebrows lifted. “Who is in charge of defining the task?”

Soldar pulled at his sleeve. “The father and uncles of the boy devise the task, so the youth is well-tested, but not required to do an impossible thing.” He returned her gaze. “The harder the task, the more status is gained at its completion.”

“But why are you telling us all of this?” Jackal interrupted impatiently. “What does this have to do with the theft of the Ring of Rosin?”

Soldar held up a hand and turned to the Swordsman. The tall, muscular man was not only an expert in the art of swordplay but also Tamadar, the leader of the Sepharim, members of which possessed the supernatural power called *dynamis* and were pledged to use their powers to protect the people of Elayas. “You know the political situation involving the unsettled territory and the challenge the Kargoliths are planning, yes?”

The Swordsman slowly nodded. His eyes took on a guarded look. “I am aware.”

“Perhaps Prince Hamideh’s manhood journey will involve suppressing that challenge. He will soon inherit the Kargolith problem. What better way to deal with the challenge than through the guise of a traditional ritual?”

“But how can he...” The Swordsman’s voice trailed off. Then, abruptly, he stood a little taller. “Ahhh...I see,” the big man nodded. “It’s possible.”

Rugal looked from Soldar to the Swordsman, allowing his exasperation to creep into his voice. “What are you talking about? I am more confused than when we first started this conversation.” His eyes tightened. “And I also want to know what this has to do with the theft.” His expression grew determined and his voice firm. "We need to get the Ring of Rosin back."

"Agreed," the Swordsman soothed Rugal. "However, the situation is more complex than it seems, with political ramifications that must be considered." The big man rubbed the back of his neck and squinted his eyes, pausing to think for a moment. He finally sighed and glanced at Soldar, who nodded.

The Swordsman cleared his throat. "The Sepharim are already involved. We have known about the Kargoliths and their desire to have their own territory and have people in the field in an attempt to understand their intentions."

"Why the secrecy?" Rugal asked, trying to keep any annoyance out of his voice. The Swordsman was Tamadar and, as such, warranted respect.

The Swordsman met Rugal's eyes. "No secrecy, Sire. We are just carrying out our duty to protect the people of Elayas. We monitor all the various factions along our borders. If an activity is detected that may become a cause for concern, it will be immediately brought to your attention. We are simply saving you from being spread too thin," he smiled gently.

Rugal's face turned red. "Thank you," he mumbled, dropping his shoulders. "I am grateful for your service."

"Do not be concerned, Sire," the Swordsman winked. "That is what we are here for." He directed his gaze back to Soldar. "Do you think the Ring of Rosin has anything to do with the Stone of Fire referenced in the note?"

Soldar's eyes narrowed. "Perhaps. It will be interesting to see what tasks have been devised for Prince Hamideh's manhood journey."

CHAPTER THREE

Good friends are chosen family.
~Dalbenian Saying

Rugal arose early, as was his custom lately. He slid out of bed and slipped into a simple tunic and leggings, hoping for a quick ride before having to deal with the theft of the Ring of Rosin and worrying about the mysterious note from the kingdom of Tolan. Maybe the brisk morning air would help bring clarity upon his return when he must assume the burdens of his court. He quietly eased through the door of his bedchamber and padded down the hall, scanning the castle interior for any signs of awakening. Going through a side entrance, he breathed easier, having avoided being stopped by an advisor or castle guardian for some kingly duty. Having free time was an infrequent occurrence when one was king.

Heading briskly for the stable and his favorite horse, a

strong muscular bay named Tag, Rugal's face split into a grin as his friend Tonar led Tag out, saddled and ready along with his own mount, a slim black mare known for her fleetness. He was so glad Tonar had taken up residence at the castle to fulfill Rugal's commission of paintings for the castle's main hall.

"Tonar, good morning," Rugal said cheerfully. "And what good timing you have. Thanks, but how did you know I wanted to ride?"

"I had a feeling," Tonar replied slyly, grinning in return. "I heard about the ring," he continued more solemnly. "Rumors are flying all over the castle."

"I'm not surprised," Rugal's face darkened momentarily. "A member of the castle staff found it missing."

"So, it's true then," Tonar questioned, his blonde hair swept back and his eyebrows furrowed.

"Yes, it's true. Soldar thinks there may be a connection between the missing ring and the kingdom of Tolan," Rugal said before hastily adding, "but keep that to yourself." He shook his head, his smile returning, and his dark brown eyes flashed mischievously. "But enough about the ring." He put his foot into the bay's stirrup and swung gracefully onto its back, taking the reins in hand. He urged the bay into a run as Tonar, laughing, leapt onto his own saddle to give chase.

An hour later, the two friends, king and artist, dismounted in front of the stables and handed their reins to a stable boy to walk the horses and cool them down.

Rugal felt much more content after his ride and entered the great hall in an amiable mood. Tonar dissolved into laughter as Treble came flying at them and landed on Rugal's arm, squawking indignantly at having been left behind. One of the few flutebirds left in existence, Treble's body was the size of Rugal's hand and bright blue in color. Musically inclined like all of his kind, he could sing with a flute-like sound. Flutebirds often played pleasing accompaniments with the people they chose to befriend. Rugal had found Treble injured and nursed him back to health. Ever since, they had been almost inseparable.

"Okay, okay, Treble, I'm here," Rugal laughed. Noting the flutebird's hurt look, he laughed again and then quickly apologized. "Sorry, Treble. We didn't mean to leave you behind." He reached out and gently scratched the soft feathers on Treble's outstretched head. Apparently satisfied, Treble scrambled up to his customary perch on Rugal's shoulder and began to preen his feathers.

Tonar watched, mesmerized by the little bird. "It's amazing," he murmured. "He seems to understand everything you say."

"Sometimes I think so," Rugal agreed. "Treble is very smart. I..." further conversation was interrupted as the Swordsman rounded the corner in front of them. His experienced eyes noted the horsehair on their leggings, and he grinned.

"So, you got an early morning ride in, eh? It's a good day for it," he said pleasantly. He was dressed in an exercise tunic and carried a broadsword casually by his side. "I was just on my way to the practice yard. It's entirely different with Oldag gone. He didn't have to maintain a castle garrison since he depended almost solely on his evil magic for defense. A few guards and his followers were about it." He flashed a grin, easing the effect his huge frame typically evoked. "We've got lots of eager volunteers, though. They all need training, but most importantly, they each have a heart to serve Elayas. I can teach the rest of what they'll need."

Rugal gazed warmly at his advisor and mentor. It was the Swordsman who taught him how to use the Sword of Fate, and without that knowledge, he wouldn't have survived. But besides that, he was also a good friend. Even more, he had become family. "Thank you for your help, Swordsman," he replied, his voice tinged with respect.

"Glad to do it, Sire," the Swordsman smiled affectionately at the young king. "Oh, by the way, Jackal asked me if I ran into you this morning, to remind you that today is a court day. Your presence will be required to judge cases beginning in the first hour after lunch." He paused. "By your leave, Sire."

Rugal shook his head uneasily. It was hard for all of them to follow court etiquette since his introduction to most of them had been prior to his ascending the throne, some even before Rugal himself knew who he really was. But he supposed Soldar was right. He recalled those long nights of study. *Was it only a few weeks ago*, Rugal wondered, *when Soldar had impressed upon me the need for proper court etiquette and diplomacy?* Rugal sighed as Soldar's voice pressed into his mind.

"It is imperative," Soldar began in his head, *"for a sovereign to engage in the formalities of court behavior to maintain the respect of his subjects and other countries. You do, after all, represent the kingdom of Elayas, your majesty."*

Rugal sighed and looked at the Swordsman, who smiled sympathetically.

"That will be fine, Tamadar," Rugal responded formally. The Swordsman winked and bowed, then continued on his way. "And I best get back to painting," Tonar interjected hurriedly. "By your leave, Sire." With a mischievous grin, he gave a quick bow and didn't wait for Rugal's response, moving quickly to follow the Tamadar out.

After spending a morning session with Soldar reviewing Tolan's historical response to past challenges to their throne and a refresher on their current border policies, Rugal was glad for a diversion as the noon hour approached. Excusing himself from further study, he went seeking Lissa and found her in the castle courtyard. He grabbed her hand and pulled her next to him on one of the ornate benches that had been scattered throughout the now-manicured lawn, providing serene spots to linger.

"You look absolutely beautiful," he murmured, gazing at her as he gently reached over to stroke her soft and shiny hair falling about her shoulders.

Lissa turned and smiled warmly at her betrothed. Rugal leaned over and embraced her, finding her lips for a sweet kiss. Lissa returned his gaze with love in her eyes, enjoying the feel of his muscular arms around her. "Your eyes light my soul..."

"Ahem," Melad cleared his throat, his face as red as his head steward badge that adorned his shirt, standing a few yards away.

Lissa pulled away from Rugal, and they both turned toward Melad, their faces flushed. Lissa giggled.

"Yes, Melad," Rugal straightened his shoulders, struggling to regain his composure.

Melad pretended not to notice his discomfort. "You are wanted in the dining hall, Sire. Court will be held in the throne room directly after lunch, which is about to be served."

Lissa jumped up, pulling Rugal up with her. "Thank you, Melad, I am absolutely famished," she grinned, tugging for Rugal to follow. The two held hands as they obediently followed the steward back into the castle.

"A MESSENGER IS RIDING IN," came the excited shout as a young boy burst into the main hall where Rugal was holding court. All heads turned as a brightly clothed page, newly appointed in the restoration of the old court traditions, proudly approached the throne where Rugal sat, interrupting a farmer's petition for more land. Rugal smiled patiently at Farin, just approaching his tenth birthday and taking his duties very seriously. He bowed breathlessly to Rugal, then, looking around, realized he had interrupted the proceedings. He began to stutter an apology, but Rugal nodded his head, motioning Farin to deliver his message.

The young boy cleared his throat and trying to suppress his excitement, announced, "The guards have received a messenger riding in as fast as his horse could carry him. He has requested a private audience to discuss a matter of great importance but will not reveal who sent him."

The Swordsman and Jackal exchanged glances with Rugal, who sat up taller on the throne's seat. Apologizing to the distraught farmer, he promised to review the farmer's case and frame a reply by noon the following day. Standing up and dismissing his court, Rugal instructed Farin to see to the messenger's comfort and provide him with a repast while he awaited further instructions.

"Perhaps we should all gather in the library," suggested the Swordsman.

Rugal walked over to the remaining men. "Good idea." He turned to his father. "Please ask Mura, Lissa, and Tonar to join us there. After our messenger friend has had a chance to eat, we will hold an audience with him there, and find out what this is all about."

"Yes, Sire," Jackal replied. "Perhaps Soldar would be a welcome addition as well? He has not left yet, and his knowledge may prove invaluable."

"Yes, of course," Rugal replied, smiling briefly. "It's good to have the support of my counselors. It makes the burden of kingship lighter." Jackal squeezed his son's shoulder affectionately before heading out the doors of the throne room.

THIRTY MINUTES LATER, they were all seated in the library, looking attentively at the messenger, a slim, proud youth about Rugal's age possessing the distinctly dark, handsome features of a citizen of Tolan.

Dressed in riding leathers, the youth had thick black hair and the beginnings of a beard. He bowed formally from the waist, and with Rugal's nod of acknowledgment, he began to recite his message:

"I, Johan of Sharvindar, in the name of King Handerbin of the kingdom of Tolan, bear greetings from my sovereign and wishes of health and happiness to the esteemed royal family of Elayas. News of Oldag's overthrow and the restoration of King Rugal, rightful sovereign of Elayas, in accordance to her laws and traditions, has brought us great joy. Our sorrow has been long in knowing that the evil king Oldag's birthplace was Tolan, and it gladdens us that he has finally met with justice." Johan paused for breath, and his listeners leaned forward in anticipation of his words.

"We wish to reassure you of our good intentions. Long have our countries viewed each other with mistrust, kindled by Oldag's rebellion. We are also aware of the theft of the Ring of Rosin, and we believe that those responsible are members of the Kargoliths, who have come to inhabit what has been the unsettled territory of Tolan, earmarked for future expansion."

"How did you know?" Rugal interrupted. "About the Ring of Rosin?"

Johan met Rugal's gaze squarely. "King Rosin had the ring made by one of the most skilled craftsmen in all of Tolan. It is a fragment from the stone of fire."

Mura nodded. "That makes sense. I know my cousin had made a special commission for its creation. I was never told the exact details, but that it arrived from a mysterious location. I remember the day it was shown at court for the first time."

Rugal's voice sharpened. "That still doesn't explain..."

"We intercepted a message from the Kargoliths, which is what prompted King Handerbin to send me here." Johan hesitated, leaning forward. "The leader of their tribe has the Ring of Rosin. King Handerbin has sent me to help you retrieve it. You will need a guide, someone familiar with Tolan."

"Just what are you proposing?" Jackal stood up, shoulders tense.

The Swordsman put up a hand. "It's okay, Jackal. It makes sense." He glanced at Soldar, who nodded. "The Kargoliths have been searching for the shards of the stone of fire for many years. It is woven into their history. Fables of old, when the wondrous bird captured it and flew to the mountains, are told around their campfires from one generation to the next. If they have the Ring of Rosin..."

"They will not give it up. This is the Year of Wisdom and the Day of Questioning approaches. They will demand King Rugal's presence." Johan looked significantly at Rugal. "For only he will be able to activate its power on that day."

Rugal cocked his head. "Day of Questioning? I have no idea what you are talking about."

Soldar cleared his throat. "An oversight on my part, Sire. We did not cover the fables of the Kargoliths, as I saw no need." He glanced at Johan and raised his eyebrows. "Perhaps I was mistaken."

"It certainly seems relevant now, Soldar," Rugal let out a noisy breath. "Please explain."

His eyes contemplative, Soldar exhaled. He turned his attention to the dark youth, and Johan nodded almost imperceptibly. Soldar turned back to Rugal.

"The Ring of Rosin has a property that no one knows about. It has been entwined in the lore of Tolan and the Kargoliths for many years and is thought to be conjecture. Apparently, that is not the case, or it would not have been stolen. Not only does it identify the true king of Elayas, but it also imparts wisdom to the king." Soldar paused and rubbed his eyes. "The Kargoliths must know the Ring of Rosin has this power."

Johan spread out his hands. "You are correct, Soldar." He bowed his head briefly. "But there is more to the fable." He continued with a storytelling inflection to his words, "The rightful king of Elayas will be able to ask the Ring of Rosin anything he desires, and the ring will impart that knowledge to him, but only once in every ten years. This day is designated as the Day of Questioning."

Rugal's eyes narrowed. "Anything? Even another person's most deeply held secrets?"

"Yes, indeed," Johan agreed. "Which is why it is so powerful. But it will only respond to the queries of the King of Elayas, and only for the Time of Sun Shadow on the Day of Questioning. This is when the sun is completely engulfed in shadow, but only for a few minutes. It is as if it is nighttime, yet it is still day."

The room remained quiet as everyone contemplated the ramifications of what had just been revealed. Finally, Rugal rubbed his cheek. "So, they stole the ring in anticipation of the Day of Questioning. But what good will it do them without me?"

"Exactly," Johan replied. "That is why I am here."

CHAPTER FOUR

"Sometimes you must rise to the challenge despite the risk.
The key is to know when to do so."
~ Janar–Master of the Sepharim, to his students

Raising his eyebrows, Rugal sat back in his chair and played with the table's edge. His gaze sharpened as he considered the foreign youth. "Please elaborate."

"Certainly, Sire," Johan drew a deep breath. "I come at the behest of my king with an invitation. We are certain the Kargoliths will attempt to kidnap you." He blinked, and his voice took on a pleading note.

"You must accompany me to Tolan."

A stunned silence greeted his words, quickly interrupted by the alarmed chatter of everyone in the room.

Rugal finally stood up. "Please quiet down. Let us hear the emissary from Tolan out."

"Thank you, Sire," Johan cleared his throat. "I know it

sounds absurd, but the best chance you have of recovering the Ring of Rosin is to confront the Kargoliths from a position of strength. In order to do that, you will have to enter into their sacred court and demand the Rite of Reciprocity. They will be unable to refuse you."

Rugal swept the hair back from his forehead and frowned. "You have lost me again. Please explain."

"The Kargoliths are a nomadic people. They have developed a method of law that is carried out by their tribal leaders in a sacred court that is held every new moon, at the center of their encampment. If a non-Kargolith requests the Rite of Reciprocity, the Kargoliths are duty-bound to treat them as they would one of their own."

"How would that help me regain the Ring of Rosin?" Rugal's brow wrinkled, and he crossed his arms.

Johan stood his ground. "The Kargoliths stole the ring. You could accuse them of the theft and demand its return."

Rugal's jaw dropped, and he shook his head. "You are telling me the same people who want to kidnap me will allow me to enter their camp untouched and will consent to my demand for the ring's return?"

"Only if you can reach the sacred circle first," Johan replied. "Otherwise, they will capture you, and you will be completely at their mercy."

"So why is this a good idea?" Rugal asked, anger creeping into his voice. "It seems to me that the risk is enormous."

Johan nodded his agreement, his cheeks flushing red. "Because the alternative is worse. You are in danger even now. If you act, you will force their hand and be in a position to demand your own terms." He drew a shaky breath. "If you remain here, they will find you. We have reason to believe that men have already been sent and are two days' ride from Cargoa. It is imperative you leave in the morning."

Rugal's eyes flashed with indignation. "I will not be coerced to leave my own castle by a mere threat from a little-known tribe bent on using me for their own gain."

Johan's fists clenched as he fought for composure. He took a calming breath. "I understand, Sire. I would feel much the same way. But I can't stress their determination enough. The Day of Questioning only comes once every ten years. If you have any hope of regaining the Ring of Rosin and avoiding the Kargolith operatives, you must make the journey to Tolan. We understand the Kargoliths and can assist you in its recovery."

Rugal gazed piercingly at Johan. "But why does Tolan care what happens to me? Why desire my recovering the Ring of Rosin?"

"Because as long as the ring remains in the hands of the Kargoliths, they pose a danger to Tolan and to Elayas," Johan replied. "If they are able to use its powers during the Time of Sun Shadow, they could gain the knowledge they need to take territory from the land on our borders."

Rugal turned to the Swordsman. "You have been monitoring the Kargoliths. What do you think?"

The big man rubbed his chin. "Our people in the field have not reported anything unusual. Except..." he paused, searching his memory. "There was mention of a tribal elder meeting at their sacred court out of their normal meeting cycle. My people didn't think it was a concern, since the Kargoliths are nomadic, and any number of things could have prompted it."

The Swordsman's eyes took on a contemplative look. "We don't have anyone close enough to participate in their meetings, so we can't be sure what it was about. The timing was about a week ago, which does speak to the possibility of a planning session regarding the theft of the ring and kidnapping you." He sighed. "Or it could have simply been about the location of their next encampment in response to the weather..."

Rugal sat listening carefully, then closed his eyes. He was relieved to find that the once familiar urge to run away when presented with a problem was replaced with something quite different–the urge to run toward it. How strange to have to control the impulse to charge ahead, rather than to flee. He smiled to himself. Felan was right. He had overcome his habit of running away just as Felan said he would.

Rugal rubbed his eyes. He missed his mentor, who had been like a father to him, and Rugal wondered how Felan would advise him now. He opened his eyes and looked around at the expectant faces. His eyes rested briefly on his beloved Lissa. Her body tilted toward him, her hazel eyes glowed with a mix of affection and curiosity. His gaze returned to Johan, who was fidgeting with his sleeve, his jaw clenched.

Rugal let out a noisy breath. "We'll leave in the morning, as Johan has suggested." He turned toward Tonar. "Please plan on accompanying us." He looked around the room again. "I will need your wisdom if this trip is to be successful. Let's get to work."

THREE HOURS LATER, Rugal leaned back in his chair and stretched. "I think we have covered everything we need for my upcoming journey. All we have left is to provide an answer for poor farmer Zelot." He couldn't help but grin. "He was most distressed when our young Farin interrupted his well-rehearsed speech."

"I have studied his case," Jackal spoke up. "It seems to me

he is within his rights. He has promised to add twenty people at fair wages and raise his contribution to the poor."

"Please take care of it for me, Father," Rugal replied. "Is there anything else?"

Murmurs of negation met his question, and he stood up briskly. "Then, if you'll excuse me and my lady, we have things to see to." Lissa took his offered hand.

"Of course, Sire," the Swordsman said smoothly. "I believe we can handle any further details. Tonar, if you wouldn't mind staying, I can give you a more complete briefing of your responsibilities," he added.

Tonar nodded his assent, and Rugal and Lissa took their leave, eager to spend time together before they would have to part. They stopped by the kitchen, where a startled cook hurriedly packed them a picnic dinner, and they headed to the stables.

"Do you think Rugal will be safe?" Mura asked Jackal as they walked the castle grounds in the evening twilight.

Jackal drew Mura closer to him. "I think so. The hardest part of being a parent, I am finding, is releasing our child. We must let him make his own decisions and fulfill his own destiny. We can't do it for him." He laughed briefly. "Although most parents don't have a king as their offspring."

Jackal pointed up at the sky. "We have to allow him to reach toward that shining star, just like in Ethiod's 'Song of Stargazer.' Now that he is king, he is Elayas." He pulled away so he could gaze into his beloved's eyes and softly sang:

Reaching toward that shining star
We have to follow long and far
But it will lead us home again
Where our hearts will finally mend

Come Elayas, follow that star
Come Elayas, come home again
To the joy at our journey's end
Bring your beauty home again

Mura sighed. "Such a beautiful song. I know you're right, Jackal. He will come home again. It just feels like I am losing him a second time."

Jackal put his hand on her cheek and rubbed the tear that had started to travel down it. "You'll never lose him, my sweet Mura. You carry him in your heart, and you are in his."

Streaks of light began to permeate the dim morning sky. Rugal and Tonar studied the packs lying on the ground, trying to think of anything else they might need.

"Are you bringing the Sword of Fate or the Key of Power?" Tonar asked, eyebrows raised.

"I have been thinking about that," Rugal glanced over at his friend. "I want to, but I think it would be too risky to bring them. My sword would give away my identity the first time I drew it. And I already lost the Key of Power once, at the most inopportune time," he gave a rueful grin.

Tonar had not been there to witness Rugal's final battle against Oldag, but the details had been enshrined in songs that had been written and were being sung across Elayas to celebrate his victory. When Rugal lost the Key of Power in the midst of the battle, success seemed out of his grasp. Lissa risked her life to come to his aid and almost died in the attempt. He shook his head. "I see what you mean. Perhaps you can borrow a sword from the Swordsman."

Rugal grinned. "You read my mind." Before he could say anything further, the Swordsman walked up, holding a sword in its sheath.

"I read your mind as well," he laughed, holding the sheath out to Rugal.

Rugal accepted it with a grateful smile. "Thank you for always looking out for me, Swordsman."

"My pleasure, Sire," the Swordsman winked and slapped Rugal on the back. "As I recall, you have other weapons that are quite formidable. Not everyone can turn into a bear. Keep your head, and you will be fine." He turned to Tonar, "Make sure to keep an eye on Johan. I inquired about him with my people in the field, and they couldn't find anything specific about him. Sharvindar is a broad region in Tolan, so that doesn't tell us much. We don't know exactly what his role is within their kingdom."

Tonar nodded solemnly. "I will do my best."

"That's all I can ask," the Swordsman grinned. He leaned down and grabbed the packs. "Best get the horses. We need to get you out of here before the castle wakes up."

Johan chose that moment to appear, with their three horses in tow. "Good morning, Sire, Swordsman, Tonar," he managed a half bow while holding the reins. "The stable boy was so kind as to direct me to your mounts. The faster we get on our way, the better."

Rugal and Tonar looked at Johan, then at the Swordsman. The big man rubbed his cheek. "I think Johan is right, Sire. Time is of the essence." Rugal took the reins from Johan and positioned the big bay so that the Swordsman could tie his pack in place behind his saddle. Rugal finished adjusting Tag's girth while the Swordsman turned his attention to Tonar's mount. Soon, all three young men were mounted, reining their horses in as they pranced in the cool predawn air. Johan's dun-colored mount was more compact but very sturdy. It snorted and jerked its head at Tag and Tonar's black mare, but settled immediately and swiveled its ears to listen when Johan said something softly to it.

"Swordsman," Rugal leaned toward the big man. "Please watch over Lissa for me while I am gone, as well as my kingdom."

The Swordsman patted his leg. "Don't worry, Rugal, we all will," he reassured the young man. "Mura, especially, will be with Lissa, giving her support."

Rugal nodded, satisfied, as Tonar, then Johan, shook hands with the Swordsman from their saddles.

"Keep your wits about you, young sirs. My field operatives have confirmed the movement of which Johan spoke. At least one party of Kargoliths have been spotted journeying toward Cargoa last night. You will need to travel quickly and take a circuitous route to avoid detection."

The dark, handsome youth, dressed in riding leathers, pulled his horse around and gazed at them with a serious expression. "That does not surprise me, Swordsman," Johan inclined his head respectfully. "Fortunately, I have studied the routes available to us in preparation for my journey here. I believe we can navigate a way around the incoming Kargoliths."

"A most excellent plan," the Swordsman commented. He turned and laid his hand on Rugal's horse. Something in the Swordsman's eyes made Rugal lean over, so that the big man could whisper something in his ear. Listening intently, Rugal gave a firm nod, then straightened in the saddle. Johan and Tonar dared not inquire what had passed between the Tamadar and the King of Elayas.

The two shook hands, and the Swordsman stepped back and raised his hand in farewell. Johan moved his horse to take the lead, Rugal falling in behind, and Tonar bringing up the rear. They didn't quite get past the manicured castle grounds when a blue object streaked by Tonar's horse and landed on Rugal's shoulder, scolding him with angry chirps at being left behind.

Rugal sighed. "It's okay, Treble. I thought it best that you stay with Lissa." He gently stroked the agitated flutebird's head in an effort to calm him down.

Treble gently nibbled Rugal's ear, let out a sigh, and fluffed his feathers. Remaining perched on Rugal's shoulder, he made it clear that he was going to stay where he was. Rugal looked apologetically at Johan and Tonar. "I don't think I can convince him to go."

Tonar grinned. "You've known what I think about Treble from the first day we met, Rug...I mean, Sire. I'm glad to have him along."

"I thought you would feel that way, Tonar. And please, while it is just us, there is no need for formality. We met when I was just Rugal and not yet king. In fact, perhaps we should come up with another name so that I can't be readily identified when we run across others."

Before Tonar could respond, Johan turned in his saddle to see what Rugal was talking about. He jerked his head back, his eyes wide, and he let out a gasp. His voice shook. "It's a Vellaquar!!" He pulled his horse to a stop and gazed in wonder at the blue flutebird. Treble returned his gaze briefly, then started preening his feathers. "How is it that a Vellaquar chooses to stay on your shoulder?"

Rugal reined his horse in and studied Johan with a puzzled expression, as Tonar's horse also came to a stop. "What is a

Vellaquar?" Rugal tried to keep the impatience he was feeling out of his voice.

Johan took a calming breath. "The rarest of birds that have been sighted in the mountains of Tolan. The bird on your shoulder looks exactly like that wondrous creature, except much smaller."

Rugal smiled. "Treble has many talents. I wouldn't be surprised if he was descended from them. He has chosen me and stays with me because we are friends." He blinked and shook his head. "But enough about Treble. We better keep going if we are going to reach our camp by nightfall."

Johan nodded. "Vellaquar, it can only be," he muttered to himself. He regarded Rugal with a new respect, tinged with awe. Regaining his composure, he turned in his saddle and urged his horse forward. The sky began to lighten as the three resumed their journey, each wrapped in their own thoughts.

CHAPTER
FIVE

A warm welcome refreshes the heart.
~ Saying of the village of Laran

"A name, we must decide on a name!" Rugal called out cheerfully. The three horses had settled into a steady trot, and they had already left the forests surrounding Cargoa behind. "How about Yandin?" Tonar suggested. "I am sure our future castle blacksmith wouldn't mind, and the name is common enough, after all."

"Yandin it is," Rugal laughed. "At least it will be easy to remember." Tag jumped playfully, responding to his rider's lighthearted demeanor. The three rode companionably through the countryside, talking about horses, hunting, and other subjects of common interest until the sun was high overhead.

"At least we don't have to worry about gormalins anymore," Tonar remarked out loud to no one in particular.

"What are gormalins?" Johan tilted his head. Now that they had cleared the forested paths, the three rode abreast. As the hours of travel wore on, their preoccupation with their own thoughts disappeared, and sharing knowledge was a welcome distraction.

Rugal cleared his throat. "Gormalins are long, sleek, black creatures with wicked teeth and claws. They are known for their ability to appear almost instantly in packs. Very few people have survived their attacks," he explained, not adding that he, Jackal, and the Swordsman were part of those few.

"So why don't you worry about them anymore?" Johan asked, glancing about alertly.

"They were a product of Oldag's reign," Tonar spoke up. "They somehow disappeared when he died," he added, then mentally kicked himself for his insensitivity. Considering Oldag had also come from Tolan, he was a subject best avoided.

Johan nodded. Realizing Tonar's sudden discomfiture and the cause of it, he diplomatically changed the subject. Coming upon a sparkling stream shaded by trees, Rugal finally drew to a halt.

"Let's rest the horses here and have some lunch," Rugal suggested, dismounting as Tonar and Johan voiced their agreement. The young men unsaddled their horses, dropping the reins so they could graze. Tonar and Rugal unpacked a simple lunch of dried meat and cheese, and the three sat together cross-legged on the ground, sharing the simple meal. Treble flew from where he had been perching in a nearby tree and onto Rugal's chest.

Rugal laughed, brushing his hair out of his eyes. "We'll leave soon, don't worry," he told the small bird, who cocked his head inquisitively at him. Johan shifted slightly, moving closer. He looked at Treble, the awe in his eyes returning.

"This is truly a wondrous thing," he exclaimed, startling Rugal with the force of his comment. Rugal raised his eyebrows, and Johan continued, "Vellaquar means *sky* in our ancient tongue. It is Vellaquar that brought us the stone of fire." His eyes gleamed. "Vellaquar is sacred to my people." He reached a hand out and carefully scratched Treble's chest, smiling as the bird fluffed his feathers and leaned toward him, tweeting softly. He gazed into the distance and continued to speak, as if to himself. "Vellaquar brought us the power to rule ourselves. That same power can help us secure our territory," his voice dropped to a whisper, "if we can but find it again."

Noting Rugal's and Tonar's confused looks, Johan shook his head. "You must forgive me, my friends, but the legends are sacred, and now is not the proper time to reveal them. Be assured that Vellaquar will be welcomed in my country, and your own status will increase a thousand-fold by his presence."

Rugal, sensing Johan would say nothing further, nodded reluctant agreement. He and Tonar would just have to wait until they met with King Handerbin to satisfy their curiosity. But another thought intruded in Rugal's mind. Johan's bearing, manner, and educated way of speaking pointed to more than just a simple messenger. There was almost certainly more to him than what met the eye.

They mounted and traveled northward through green hills and valleys. Riding at a steady pace, the mystery of Johan and Vellaquar occupied Rugal's thoughts. Their destination was a small village in the north-central portion of Elayas, where they planned to find lodging.

As evening approached, they rode up a hill, and ascending the rise, an inhabited area came into view. No walls were evident, but a high tower guaranteed the presence of a guardsman, even though their wariness had been greatly reduced since Oldag's defeat. A dirt road welcomed a direct approach, stretching toward the hills.

"That must be Laran," Rugal stated confidently. "We'll pass through both Laran and Kepath on our way, according to the Swordsman." He smiled at Johan. "I think you will find our villagers quite friendly to visitors. The more isolated villages don't receive guests very often, and it is an excuse to show off their hospitality. They are great ones for tradition, some of which are quite interesting."

"I would like to meet your countrymen," Johan replied eagerly. "I think in some ways, we are not so different, if we could only get to know each other."

Tonar bobbed his head in agreement, then cleared his throat. "Uhhhh, Rugal..." he began.

Sensing something in Tonar's voice, Rugal pulled on the reins to stop Tag and shifted in his saddle, giving his friend his full attention.

Tonar rubbed his cheek. "I think it would be a good idea if you tucked Treble out of sight. He's liable to make quite a stir, and we are supposed to be ordinary youths, traveling to see relatives."

"Thanks for reminding me," Rugal agreed, tucking Treble inside his shirt. Treble, sensing the need for secrecy, remained quiet. Rugal touched his heels to Tag's sides and started down the hill toward the village at a walk, with Tonar and Johan on either side of him.

A MAN TROTTING his chestnut horse on the road approached the three youths. As he neared, his confident bearing and his salt-and-pepper hair made him seem a person of consequence.

Coming within hailing distance, he called out, "Welcome to Laran, young fellows." He sidled his horse up to theirs, his eyes quickly looking over the youths, and he relaxed a fraction in his saddle. Smiling politely, he continued, "My name is Mubarak. Might I inquire about your business in Laran? We do not wish to intrude on your privacy, but Oldag's legacy of fear lingers, despite the ascendancy of good King Rugal."

Tonar, realizing he would serve best as their spokesman since he was closest to the ordinary youths they wished to appear as, smiled at the stocky older man. "Greetings to you, sir," he replied cheerily. "I am Tonar, and these are my cousins," he paused for a moment, thinking quickly. "Yandin and Jolan. We are on our way to Farath to visit relatives. We were hoping to find lodging in your town and plan on resuming our journey in the morning."

Mubarak nodded. "We would be honored to have you as our guests. Although we are not large enough to have an inn, we do have a guesthouse where you'll be made welcome." He gestured toward the village, where they could see simple structures and children playing in the streets. "You are fortunate. Today is something of a holiday. Our community hall is hosting our annual summer dance tonight, and you are welcome to attend." He winked and smiled. "I daresay there will be some pretty dance partners available."

"What are you celebrating?" Johan-Jolan asked, stroking his horse's neck as he looked curiously at Mubarak.

The older man stroked his chin and chuckled. "One excuse is as good as another when it comes to a community gathering, but tonight, we are celebrating the fruits of our labor for the past year."

He pointed toward the fields surrounding the village and the grove of fruit trees in the distance. "We're simple farmers, you see. And we have been very fortunate in this year's harvest.

Rugal's brave fight in overthrowing Oldag and our security for the coming winter season with our fine crops, gives us much reason to celebrate. You are all welcome to share our joy."

Mubarak's gaze swept them again. "But come, follow me, and I'll show you to our guesthouse," he said, turning his horse to go back toward the village, the three companions urging their own horses to follow.

"A FAIRLY CORDIAL WELCOME," Rugal commented, as the three of them washed the dust from their trip in the guestroom bath. They had seen to their horses and looked forward to an evening of relaxation. Mubarak had shown them to a simple but quite adequate room. Thick rugs covered its rough wood floor. An extra cot had been set up, in addition to the two beds in an adjoining room, where Treble quietly napped. A small fireplace and a table with chairs that they now occupied completed the main room. Each had brought a fresh tunic and leggings in their packs, which they changed into.

A knock on the door caused Rugal to jump up, but the smells wafting into the room relieved any suspicion, and he opened the door to a young boy carefully balancing a tray set with roast, bread, and cheese, along with a jug of ale. Bringing the tray to the table, he bore a close resemblance to Mubarak. Remembering his manners, the boy smiled at the guests, his eyes bright with curiosity.

"Hello, I am Silar," he said. "My uncle Mubarak asked me to inform you that the dance will begin in two hours. I will return to escort you there, if you wish."

Rugal nodded in return, gratified to see he had guessed

correctly. "Thank you, Silar," he replied. "We would be honored by your escort."

The boy grinned. "It will be fun–you'll see." He headed out the door, leaving them to their dinner. They quickly devoured the simple yet hearty meal. Tonar gathered the plates and set them aside. He cleared his throat. "I think we should try to sleep before the celebration this evening. We will have to leave early in the morning to stay on schedule."

"Tonar's right," Johan agreed, then hesitated. "But shouldn't one of us keep watch?" Seeing the expression on Tonar's face, he hurried to add, "I do not fear the villagers. It is the men who are seeking to capture Rugal that have my concern."

The same thought had already crossed Rugal's mind. He also knew from his studies with Soldar and the Swordsman that the Tolanese were very suspicious of any extraordinary powers such as *dynamis*. Johan knew he used his power to defeat Oldag. He took a breath. "I will handle it, Johan. Sleep without fear."

Johan looked intently at Rugal, digesting the implications of his words, then nodded slowly in agreement. "Yes," he said. "Then I shall sleep well."

Rugal and Tonar exchanged a relieved glance. Johan, acting as if nothing unusual had passed between them, lay down on the cot. Tonar, following his lead, settled into one of the beds.

Rugal walked to the door, closed his eyes, and concentrated. A warm, familiar feeling swept over him as he began to focus his power, concentrating on the Sepharim technique of sensing danger and weaving a thread of protection around them so he would be warned if someone threatened them by an intrusion on his consciousness. The Tamadar had only recently taught him the technique, and he was eager to try it.

Satisfied, he went to the other bed and lay down. Soon, all three travel-weary young men were asleep.

CHAPTER SIX

One should choose to only hate evil.
~ Tenet of the Sepharim

Two hours later, Rugal was awakened by someone's approach to the guesthouse. Pleased that his thread of protection had worked, he reached out and sensed it was Silar, just as the young boy raised his hand and knocked softly. Slipping to his feet, he saw Tonar and Johan get up as he padded to the door, opened it, and greeted Silar with a smile.

"Greetings, Silar. We were just getting up," he said, motioning for the boy to come in and sit down.

Silar smiled shyly in return. "As soon as you're ready, I'll show you to the community hall," he said, anticipation of the event evident in his voice.

"We'll be just a moment," Tonar called from the adjourning room. He checked on Treble, who continued sleeping on his perch by Rugal's bed. Then, he and Johan joined Rugal and Silar in the main room. They combed their hair neatly and made adjustments to their tunics, and with Silar assuring them they looked fine, they followed the boy out into the street.

The stars shone brightly over the small village as they made their way down the hard-packed main road. Passing various dwellings and an occasional shop, they came upon a building that stood larger than the rest, toward the center of the town.

"This is the town hall," Silar announced proudly as he led them toward the front door, where many other people were entering. The sound of music and laughter met their ears as they walked through the entrance and into a larger hall, the center of which had been cleared for a dance floor. Benches were set around the walls, and several musicians were playing on a raised platform. The back section of the hall was set up separately with heavy wooden tables filled to overflow with food and drink.

Rugal and Tonar, familiar with such dances, were eager to join in the activities. Mubarak spotted them and waved, making his way through the crowd toward them. Greeting them cheerily, he noticed Johan's wide-eyed curiosity, his head turning as he tried to see everything at once. Mubarak smiled reassuringly at the young man. Turning to include Rugal and Tonar, who were obviously at ease, he offered to show them around.

Rugal, standing erect, his long hair swept back, thought quickly. He really just wanted to observe and listen to the mood of the villagers. Besides, he wouldn't have fun dancing without Lissa, but that didn't mean Tonar and Johan couldn't enjoy themselves.

"Thank you," Rugal replied gracefully, "but I'd rather stay

back and watch a while. I'm sure Tonar and Jo...Jolan, would enjoy your offer."

Mubarak looked to Tonar and Johan, who nodded in agreement. "It's settled then," Rugal waved toward the musicians and the crowd. "I'll meet all of you later." He watched them fade into the crowd and walked to a table, pouring himself a cup of ale. Spotting a bench that would give him a good view of the dance as well as placing him within hearing of several small groups of people, he headed for it and sat down, making himself comfortable.

Many of the townspeople, dressed in brightly colored tunics and dresses, murmured polite greetings as they passed him. Although many tried to glance at him covertly, Rugal felt a surge of relief when he was not actively sought for conversation. The townspeople had come to the conclusion they had hoped for, three quite ordinary youths traveling to visit relatives.

He sat back and turned his attention to the musicians. A tall, slim man in a yellow robe stood playing a stringed instrument of honey brown. A fleeting reminder of Ethiod crossed his mind. His future father-in-law was the most famous musician of Elayas and played an instrument similar to the one that the musician gently strummed. He smiled as an image of Ethiod's grey hair and bright blue eyes welled up in his mind.

Another man was sitting on a stool playing a flute while a third sat on the floor with a variety of drums set before him. They played a quiet, soothing tune as neighbors and friends greeted each other, waiting for the signal to begin the dance music.

Sighing, he rested his back against the hard wood and began to concentrate. Not wishing to eavesdrop, he still wanted to know the general mood of his people now that he had defeated Oldag and taken his place on the throne as the rightful king of Elayas. He closed his eyes and tried to filter out the background noise, as he listened to two young men engaged in earnest conversation.

"I still say I'm moving to Lisbon," the taller one was telling his companion.

"But why would you want to?" his friend asked, obviously puzzled.

"Can't you see?" The youth said excitedly. "Now that Oldag's gone, we are free to pursue what we wish. And I can go study there!"

The boy shook his head doubtfully. "But how do you know it's really true?"

"I just do," the taller boy replied stubbornly. "And I shall go."

Hmmm, Rugal thought to himself. *So, the seeds of hope are mixed with the seeds of doubt. My reign is a big adjustment. It still needs time for old habits and old fears to dissolve completely.* He opened his eyes and looked around. Spotting two older men to his left, he strained to hear what they were saying.

"...be thankful the crops are good this year. King Rugal has restored the treasury for those whose crops were not sufficient, but I'd rather we not have to call upon it."

The other man nodded his agreement. "It's a good thing to have, though, just in case. One cannot always depend on the weather in this part of the country. I think our new king is truly concerned for the welfare of his people. He's a bit young, but I hear he's got Jackal and the Tamadar to advise him, and he is progressing well. He did kill Oldag, and that took extraordinary courage."

Taking a sip of ale, the first man scratched his chin. "I have to agree with you there," he said. "I think our Rugal," Rugal smiled at the pride that was reflected in his voice, "is a fine young man and will be a credit to the throne, if given the chance."

"Then you have no fear that he can be corrupted like Oldag?"

He shook his head, taking another sip. "Not with the Sepharim restored. And the lad did succeed to the throne through the Sepharim's laws–not by force and foul play like Oldag."

The other nodded again and then tapped his companion's shoulder and motioned to the side. "There's the ladies. I don't know about your Jula, but my Cess won't let me into the house if I'm not with her for the first dance."

Rugal stretched as the two men walked away, laughing. He went to refill his cup and bumped into a man walking quickly from the direction of the tables. The man's ale cup flew into the air, drenching Rugal's shirt front.

"I beg your pardon," the man apologized profusely. "Please allow me to get you a fresh tunic." He made a half-hearted gesture at sponging Rugal's shirt with a napkin. "My home is not far. You can change there."

Rugal took in his sandy blonde hair and piercing blue eyes. Not very tall, the man was dressed similarly to the other townspeople. While appearing clumsy, he still couldn't quite disguise a subtle grace to his movements.

Looking down at his dripping tunic and back at the man, Rugal didn't sense any danger and reminded himself he could always turn into a wolf, if needed. "I would really like to get dry. Thank you," he responded, following him out of the hall.

As the two quickly made their way down the street and out of sight of the community hall, Rugal's companion glanced over his shoulder as if looking for someone. No one was about, which seemed to satisfy him. He turned and bowed to Rugal, flashing a grin. "Good evening, Sire," he said earnestly. "I'm sorry about the ale, but I was instructed to speak with you upon your arrival. I didn't wish to disturb you in your endeavor." Rugal blushed when he realized he meant his eavesdropping. He was consoled by reminding himself that whatever happened in his kingdom was his business, since he was duty-bound to protect it. "So, I waited for you to get up," he finished.

Rugal's eyes narrowed at the man before him. "And who might you be, and who told you I would be here?"

The blonde man quickly bowed again. "I am known as Legas, and I am of the Sepharim. The Tamadar sent word a couple of days ago that you would be passing through."

Rugal sucked in a quick breath. His friend, the Swordsman, Tamadar of the Sepharim, was most meticulous in his duties. Although easygoing, he left little to chance and must have alerted the Sepharim network as soon as their plans had been made definite. It was good to know that he had a group of people working for him through the benevolence of the Sepharim, greatly simplifying the task of keeping up with conditions in all corners of Elayas. He turned his attention back to the member of the Sepharim before him now.

"And what were your instructions?" he slowly asked.

Composing himself to recite his message, Legas began. "Greetings, King Rugal of Elayas. It is my sincere hope your journey is progressing well. I must apologize for the inconvenience in how this message is being delivered, but I wished to avoid raising fears here at the castle since I was unable to catch you alone, before you left on your journey.

"Legas, my associate, is completely trustworthy, and I have instructed him to warn you of any potential danger. Some of the Sepharim have warned me that word of your journey has been leaked, and I fear of a plot to stop you before you reach Tolan.

"As you know, in some areas, hatred of Tolan is very strong

because it is Oldag's birthplace. In addition to that, some of our citizens are unduly suspicious of other cultures, and do not wish Elayas to succeed in establishing a friendship with them. You may have enemies from within and from the Kargoliths pursuing you."

Legas took a breath before continuing, discreetly checking about to ensure no one had come upon them. "My message is this, beware of strangers, even friendly ones. Only trust Sepharim and only those who ask you in conversation, 'Have you an interest in music?' In which you reply, 'We hope to see Stargazer soon.' These people will aid you in any way they can. Be careful, young Rugal."

Rugal's first reaction was resentment at being so closely watched, but quickly, a more sensible Rugal realized it was necessary to ensure his safety as king. He was fortunate to even be able to attempt such a mission so early in his reign. He should be grateful for the Swordsman's foresight and his discretion in informing him of potential danger without unduly alarming Lissa and Mura. He gazed at Legas thoughtfully.

"I see," he said. "It seems to me we shall have to take some precautions." He smiled at the man before him. "Thank you, Legas. Your message may have saved me some future grief." He looked down at his tunic. "If not a bath," he commented wryly.

Legas grinned back and reached into his tunic, pulling out a folded bundle. He shook it out and offered it to Rugal. It was a dry tunic.

Chuckling, Rugal took his wet one off and slipped the dry one over his head. An idea struck him as he and Legas turned to make their way back towards the hall. "So, you are Sepharim?" Rugal asked Legas offhandedly as they began sauntering toward the community hall, the lights from its windows glowing invitingly against the dark of the nighttime sky.

Legas nodded in comprehension. “I do have some measure of power,” he said in a low voice.

“Good,” Rugal’s eyes brightened. He considered his next question. “Please answer me honestly, without fear,” he said. “Do you harbor any unusual prejudice towards Tolan or their people? With regard to Oldag and his evil reign, do you blame the citizens of Tolan for his rule or have a dislike for them because they are different from us?”

Legas considered Rugal’s question carefully, slowing his steps even more. He rubbed his cheek. “As a student of the Sepharim, I have been taught all people are my brothers and sisters, even if they are not Sepharim or citizens of Elayas, and I should only hate evil. Oldag was certainly evil, but that does not mean the Tolanese are.” He shrugged. “I heard they had exiled Oldag themselves and regretted his actions in Elayas. I have never met a Tolanese, but they couldn’t be that much different.” He finally shook his head. “I don’t believe so, Sire.”

Rugal dropped his shoulders and relaxed. “Good, then I have a favor to ask,” he grinned, a mischievous glint coming into his dark brown eyes. “How would you like a chance to show someone what it means to be a member of the Sepharim?”

CHAPTER
SEVEN

"May your life always shine bright in the lives of others."
~ Sepharim Life Force Ceremony

A few minutes later, Rugal and Legas slipped through the doors and into the dance hall. They separated, and Rugal grinned when he spotted both Tonar and Johan partnered with two young women. Johan was watching his partner as she taught him the steps of the boisterous dance. He was having a hard time with the pattern and swinging of his partner but catching on quickly to the steps and rhythm. The music was just ending, and Johan and Tonar breathlessly excused themselves, their eyes shining with excitement as they made their way back toward Rugal.

"It seems you've had no trouble finding partners," Rugal commented dryly.

"It's his dark good looks," Tonar said. "All the girls think him quite mysterious."

Johan and Tonar laughed. Tonar slapped Johan on the back, and Rugal smiled approvingly at the easy camaraderie that had developed between the two. Maybe Tonar could solve the mystery of Johan. The more he was with him, the more certain Rugal grew that Johan was more than a simple messenger.

"The dances are different in my country," Johan said in a low voice, but the spirit of celebration is the same. He glanced at the girls who were getting cold drinks. "It was very enjoyable," he said, "learning a new way to dance. In my country, the women are too shy to dance with a stranger. They either must dance with a relative or a trusted friend."

Rugal nodded. With a flash of insight, he realized that although emotions were universal, there could be many ways to express them, none necessarily better than others. An important thing to understand if one was to do what Johan was doing. And Johan was handling these new situations very well. He hoped Johan would handle what Rugal had planned in the next hour as well as he handled the dance. The more they knew about each other, the more sympathetic to each other they would be. At least, Rugal hoped so.

"So, where have you been?" Tonar asked. "I saw you leave with another man a little while ago."

Rugal glanced about to make sure no one was listening. "The Swordsman arranged a message for us. Sorry to cut your fun short, but we need to meet in our room in about thirty minutes."

Sensing the urgency in Rugal's voice, the other two nodded in unquestioning agreement. Rugal allowed himself a small smile. "Now go dance while you can," he ordered. "We have appearances to maintain."

Tonar and Johan nodded seriously, then the three of them burst out laughing. That was one order they would gladly carry out. The music started back up as they headed toward the young ladies eagerly waiting for them.

Rugal slipped back out and headed for their room to prepare for the next hour and give himself time to think. The air had turned cool, and he shivered, hurrying to the guest-house. Treble met him at the door in a flurry, scolding him for being gone so long. He scratched the flutebird affectionately, then set him on the back of one of the chairs, where he would be out of the way but could observe what was going on.

Deciding on an informal arrangement about the fireplace, Rugal placed four chairs in a semicircle, each one a knee span apart. Satisfied, he opened his pack and dug inside. He had packed carefully and sparingly, but at the last moment, he had felt compelled to add his blue robe, having a strange feeling that he would need it. He decided now would be a good time to put it on, adding more formality to the ceremony they were about to perform in an attempt to bridge the gap between Johan's culture and their own.

An image of Johan welled up in his mind, the dark youth sitting restlessly at a table, while an older man with a striking resemblance to Soldar instructed him on Elayas and the basic practices of the Sepharim. He laughed out loud, startling Treble. Rugal had sat impatiently through many similar lectures on the culture of Tolan, and only now did it have any real significance for him. He regretted not having paid closer attention, but he found reality much more interesting than theory.

Rugal shook his head wryly and slipped the bright blue robe over his head. A muffled knock on the door alerted him to Legas' presence. Tugging the robe in place, he quickly opened it, smiling, and noted a bundle of blue cloth tucked under the other man's arm.

"Thank you for coming," Rugal greeted the older man,

pleased that he had consented to join the ceremony. Seeing Legas looking about, he added, “The others will be with us soon. I left them at the hall with instructions to join us after a few more dances. I don’t want any villagers to get suspicious.”

Legas nodded approvingly at Rugal’s precautions. “Most sensible, Sire,” he agreed. “The townspeople of Laran are good, kind people, but can be rather tenacious when aroused. It is best to continue as you are to avoid any uncomfortable questions.” His sharp eyes swept the room. “I see that you’ve arranged the chairs. May I ask which ceremony you had in mind?”

“I thought that we could do the *elpise*. It’s simple, and I want to show Johan a little about our beliefs. If he can experience a brief ceremony, I think we’ll have accomplished something toward a better understanding of one another.” Rugal’s eyes sparkled at the thought. He walked to the fire and fiddled with the chair arrangement, trying to calm his excitement.

“The Tamadar is right. If anyone can forge peace, it is this strong-willed youth,” Legas muttered to himself. He smiled in agreement and raised his voice. “I think this is an excellent idea, Sire. The Tamadar took the liberty of informing me on the nature of your mission. It seems as if you have already gotten a good start.”

Rugal smiled shyly at the compliment. He was man enough to admit that he was still young and had much to learn. He also realized that the unassuming man before him must be remarkable indeed to be so high in the Swordsman’s trust. A compliment from Legas was to be valued, for as a student of the Sepharim, he had learned that compliments were never given lightly, and false flattery deemed as bad as a direct lie.

“Thank you, Legas,” he said respectfully. Further conversation was delayed by another knock at the door.

At Rugal’s nod, Legas opened the door to admit the two

youths, their cheeks still flushed from dancing and the brisk night air. Glancing curiously at Legas, Tonar and Johan politely greeted the sandy-bearded man and Rugal. Although both were impatient to find out why they were called to the guest house unexpectedly, they remained quiet in deference to Rugal's obvious desire to conduct the meeting, his enthusiasm making his dark, round eyes sparkle intensely. It was apparent he was up to something as he stood in his startingly brilliant blue robe, which he had donned instead of a red one signifying royalty.

Sepharim business would be about this night, Tonar realized and smiled. Still uninitiated in many ways to the Sepharim, his attendance at their ceremonies had stirred something in his soul. Being a Patriotes, without the gift of extraordinary power that members of the Sepharim possessed, he was still able to share in their rituals. He instinctively sensed it as an ideal way to reach Johan as well. He flashed a look of comprehension at Rugal and smiled his approval.

Rugal winked in response and gestured toward the chairs. "Why don't we sit down?" he asked pleasantly.

Johan had immediately taken notice of Rugal's ceremonial robe and covertly watched Legas shake out his bundle and slip a similar robe over his head. He carefully observed that neither robe showed any symbols of rank or identification of the wearer. Understanding something special was about to take place, Johan slipped quietly into a chair between Rugal and Tonar, with Legas to the far left, and gave Rugal his full attention as he began to speak. Rugal directed his gaze at Johan.

"Johan of Tolan, I invite you to join us in a ceremony of the Sepharim," he began formally, noting Johan's interested expression. "It is a simple one that any person who so desires may take part in. The ceremony itself is often used to introduce initiates into the Sepharim, but there is no obligation attached to it." He paused and held out his hands. "If you will all join hands."

At Rugal's quiet command, each man grasped the hand of his neighbor. Rugal and Legas, each on an end, held their outside hand in a relaxed position. They each employed preparatory techniques of readiness for the feat Rugal had in mind.

"If you will close your eyes," Rugal continued. "And think thoughts of peace. Of the ocean gently lapping the shore. Of the warmth of your own bodies as you bask in the sun. Become completely relaxed."

Legas covertly watched as Tonar and Johan obediently set their minds on restful images, their bodies relaxing and the day's tensions draining as they concentrated on Rugal's voice. Rugal glanced at Johan and Tonar, then signaled to Legas to begin.

Drawing a deep breath and exhaling slowly, Legas began the chant with practiced ease, Treble adding his sweet flute-like voice:

"Seidous Sepharim alkalfam dous mosfet sandali."

We pledge ourselves to the Sepharim and to each other.

"Seidous man shoma dynamis shod elis toujou keen."

We pledge to use our powers for good and to defend against evil.

"Seidous lisban to man shoma perciles zanten fous."

We pledge our lives to peace for ourselves and for all people.

"Chetoere cardozen merindar laison serften mia."

May your life always shine bright in the lives of others.

Johan and Tonar automatically opened their eyes, feeling a compulsion to do so as Legas finished the final words and raised his free hand upward toward Rugal. At the same moment, Rugal lifted his own free hand toward Legas. Johan, eyes wide, felt something imminent about to happen as Rugal and Legas concentrated on joining their power. A blue flash suddenly extended from Rugal's hand and an orange one from Legas'. The two forces met and joined over their heads, enveloping the room with their brilliance.

Treble, startled from his perch, flew wildly in Rugal's direction, breaking the concentration he and Legas had to maintain in order to form the forces of light. Rugal lifted his arm for Treble to land on, then sat back in his chair and sighed. He looked apologetically at Johan. "I intended to extend the ceremony, but I didn't anticipate Treble's reaction. He hasn't seen the light force before and must have wanted to assure himself that it wasn't harmful to me, which, of course, it isn't."

"Vellaquar," Johan breathed, eyeing Treble with awe. "He exhibits the characteristics of his ancestor. Loyal and protective to those he chooses," Johan nodded appreciatively. "I must admit the same thought had run through my mind until I felt the sense of peace it brought. I have never experienced such a thing before."

Legas, smoothing his beard with his right hand, grinned at Johan. "Many people haven't, but it's a perfectly natural phenomenon. You see, our guild, the Sepharim, discovered that each person—whether or not they have any special gifts of the power we call *dynamis*—has a color associated with their life force. As far as we can determine, body chemistry has a lot to do with the color, as well as genetics. However, it seems that these are not the only factors because they do not always correlate. We can also see that the color may change, which is not understood.

"The King of Elayas is the only person that has a blue life force. When it is time for the succession of the throne, the blue life force of the current king transforms to another color, and the one to succeed him has the blue life force. While we don't understand exactly how it works, we believe that is why the Ring of Rosin recognizes the true king. King Rosin commissioned the ring to have special properties that may tap into a person's life force.

"We have learned, through concentration techniques, to funnel the force through our bodies, and even to focus power through it so that it can serve as an outlet. This is the manner in which Rugal fought Oldag. Another interesting factor we have found is that people who have the same life force color seem to have a natural affinity for each other. You've probably met people you've liked instantly or felt an immediate kinship with."

Johan nodded thoughtfully.

Legas smiled. "More than likely, they have the same life force color as you do."

Fascinated, Johan turned to Tonar, who had listened attentively to Legas' lecture. "Do you know what color your life force is?" Johan asked him curiously.

Tonar shook his head. "No, but neither have I been blessed with *dynamis*, so I never had the opportunity to learn the technique." He turned hopefully to Rugal.

"Can anyone do it? I mean, discover the color of their life force?"

Glancing at Legas, who nodded, Rugal considered his answer before replying.

"Yes, Tonar. You can. We would have to get a special dispensation from the Tamadar, since neither you, nor Johan, have sworn the vows of the Sepharim."

Tonar, surprise written on his face, rubbed his fingers across the smooth arm of his chair. "Is it dangerous?" he asked nervously. "I mean, I've participated in ceremonies before, without any problems."

"No, not at all," Legas hurriedly reassured him. "It's just that, as I have said, it can be used to focus power. If you have not sworn to use your power only for the good, which is an unalterable condition that the Sepharim's tenets most rigidly state, then we cannot perform the necessary techniques.

"Tonar, we have already seen that you do not possess *dynamis*. There is no shame in that," he added quickly as Tonar bowed his head. "You contribute your talents brilliantly in ways other people can never do. But," and Legas turned back to Johan. "You are an unknown quantity. We should be able to generate enough power between Rugal and myself to bring the colors of your life force forth, at least momentarily. Since your country has not encouraged the use of these powers, we don't know whether or not you possess any *dynamis*. Our codes bind us to safeguard its use.

"If, during the ceremony, you evince any power, you must agree to swear by these codes." Legas' tone lightened. "Then, by doing so, you could benefit from the training you are eligible to receive from the Sepharim. And we would know that your power will only be used in good, beneficial ways."

Johan looked at Rugal, an unspoken question in his eyes. Rugal, brushing his hair back, sighed. Sensing Johan's question, he decided to be direct. "No, Johan. Oldag was an initiate of the Sepharim, but he never took the vows. And neither had his followers.

"If they had, the force of those vows would have compelled them to die rather than intentionally harm another human being with their power, except in self-defense. I was able to kill Oldag because, in the eyes of my sworn vows, the cause was just. The vows do not include normal abilities, it is a safeguard so that no man or woman will use their *dynamis* as an unfair advantage over another."

Before Rugal could further elaborate, Treble stretched his

wings and fluffed his feathers, regarding each one of them sleepily. Legas, who had seen Stargazer's flutebird in earlier years, had expressed no surprise at Rugal's companion but laughed now. "It seems to me your friend is telling us it's bedtime," he grinned. He got up, slipped his robe over his head, and stretched. "I best be going myself."

Rugal, Tonar, and Johan each stood up and shook his hand firmly. "Thank you for the ceremony," Johan murmured. "It was most enlightening," he added, grinning as he emphasized "light." Legas laughed, enjoying the joke. "You've learned our language quite well. I am most impressed. Good fortune to you, Johan." Johan bowed slightly from the waist, "And to you, Legas of the Sepharim. Your company has indeed been a pleasure."

Rugal and Tonar, both startled at Legas' statement, realized that he was right. Johan's native language was different from their own. He spoke with no accent, an impressive accomplishment. Rugal's opinion of the young courier increased even more, and again, he had a feeling that there was more to Johan than what met the eye.

Tonar spoke to Legas as the sandy-haired man folded his robe into a neat package. "Yes, thank you for the ceremony. I hope we meet again."

"I'm sure we will, Tonar," Legas replied easily, "I plan on being at the castle when you unveil the paintings Rugal commissioned from you for the Great Hall."

Tonar, masking his surprise that Legas knew his actual occupation, made a mental note to ask Rugal about Legas later. "I'll look forward to it," he replied gracefully.

Rugal followed Legas to the door as Tonar and Johan began to prepare for sleep. Legas' voice dropped to a whisper. "Good fortune, Sire, and remember the Tamadar's words. The Sepharim will be here for you, if you have need."

Rugal clapped the older man on the back. “Thank you, Legas. You’re a good man, and I won’t forget this,” he paused, eyebrows raised. “I expect I’ll be seeing you again.”

“You can count on it, Sire,” Legas grinned. “Good night and safe travels,” he said, then slipped out the door and into the night.

Rugal turned toward the bedroom, gently lifting Treble from his shoulder and onto the bedpost. Seeing Tonar and Johan already in their beds, he slipped out of his ceremonial robe and into his. Noting that dawn was only four hours away, he quickly wove a mental thread of protection about the guest house and soon all three companions were in a deep sleep.

CHAPTER
EIGHT

"Knot anger with knowledge."
~ The Swordsman

The morning sun gently bathed the hills as Rugal stirred from his bed. Glancing at Johan and Tonar's sleeping forms, he shook each on the shoulder, and they swiftly began to prepare for the day's journey. Eager to be on their way, they thanked Mubarak for the town's hospitality and continued their trek as the sun began to climb in the sky.

Rugal breathed in the crisp autumn air and made light conversation with Tonar and Johan. They had quickly made their way out of Laran, soon leaving its houses and cultivated fields far behind. Towards noon, they encountered a forest of deep wood. Leading northwest, the way they must go, its trees blotted out the sun. The growth thickened, forcing them to ride in single file. At times, Tonar or Johan had to dismount and hack through the underbrush pressing against the path.

Rugal felt uneasy as they traveled deeper into the forest, and Legas' message from the Tamadar to "beware of strangers" kept running through his mind.

They ate dried beef as they rode, in unspoken agreement not to stop as the forest closed around them. Treble remained unusually silent, burrowing into Rugal's chest for comfort. The hairs on the back of Rugal's neck prickled with a sense of foreboding. The horses were restless and moved nervously, shying at imaginary terrors. Tonar, tightlipped and determined, reigned his skittish mare firmly as he brought up the rear, following Rugal with Johan leading. All three remained wary and tense as they penetrated deeper into the forest, and the afternoon began to edge towards dusk.

Suddenly, Rugal's sixth sense informed him they were not alone, but by then, it was too late. The intense feeling had caused him to turn in the saddle to warn Tonar, just in time to glimpse Tonar's slim black mare rearing, her eyes rolling in fear before she bolted, crashing through the underbrush. His friend Tonar was nowhere to be seen.

"Johan!" Rugal cried out sharply as the mare's noisy departure caused the dark youth to stop and turn back to where Rugal sat his horse, his face mirroring his anxiety. "He just disappeared," Rugal gasped. "I didn't see anyone or hear anything!" He paused, fear for his friend causing his mouth to dry, and a queasy feeling invaded his stomach. "I felt a presence," he continued. "I know someone else was here. Someone has captured Tonar!"

"Are you sure he didn't fall from his horse? She has been skittish all afternoon. Perhaps Tonar fell from her back into a thick patch of brush," Johan spoke soothingly and logically. He dismounted and handed Rugal the reins of his horse. "Here, hold Raksh for me. I'll go check the trail."

Rugal accepted the reins. His *dynamis* ability would do no

good here. The forest canopy was too thick for flight, and on the ground, it was impossible to tell the direction Tonar's captors had gone. He sat on his horse, waiting, but he knew Johan wouldn't find Tonar. He feared for Tonar in that certainty, and his fear grew when Johan trudged back, his face grim.

Johan stepped up to Rugal and held up a piece of torn cloth. It was bright red, the color of Tonar's tunic. "I found this," Johan spoke, anger tinging his voice and his black eyes flashing. "There is no trace of a disturbance except for the mare's flight. And I also found this."

Johan held up an object in his left hand so that Rugal could see a thick gold chain with a medallion hanging from it. "Tonar must have torn it from his captor's neck when they turned to flee. The language on the medallion is foreign to my native tongue, but I recognize the script." His brow furrowed in anger. "It is from the Kargoliths. They have traveled more swiftly than I thought possible." His troubled eyes met Rugal's. "I think they believe they have captured you."

Rugal's heart sank at Johan's words. He numbly held his hand out, and Johan poured the chain into it.

"Apparently, they are traveling on foot, probably toward a close rendezvous where they can obtain horses. Whoever kidnapped Tonar planned it carefully. We cannot follow through the underbrush with the horses, and if we leave the horses, we will surely die, unable to find our way out. Tonar's mare is no doubt still running. I'm afraid we'll have to continue on and get out of this cursed wood. Then we can formulate a plan and provision ourselves to search for him."

"Why?" Rugal asked, glaring at Johan, anguish in his voice. "Why Tonar? He is a good man and a good friend." He pounded the cantle of his saddle with his fist in frustration. "Legas warned me to beware. I should have been more cautious."

"They surely won't hurt him," Johan reasoned. "They obviously want something and know they need you to obtain it. They have mistaken him for you."

Rugal shook his head, tears welling unbidden to his eyes. He bowed his head.

"Now, Sire," Johan started more firmly. "It was not your fault. They were very quiet and quick, obviously they knew what they were about. I know how you feel, but if we're going to help Tonar, we need to focus and equip ourselves."

Rugal swallowed and met Johan's eyes. Johan moved forward and straightened Rugal's stirrup–giving it a tug. "I miss him, too," he added, regret in his voice.

Rugal nodded, his eyes glittering with pain. He straightened in his saddle, regaining his composure completely. A king, set on justice for one of his subjects, merged with the youth determined to rescue a friend as close as a brother.

"You are right, of course, Johan," Rugal replied.

Johan, instantly noting the change in Rugal, spoke his next words tinged with respect. "Very good, King Rugal. May I suggest we move with all haste to escape this wood and seek a place in which to formulate Tonar's rescue?"

Rugal nodded curtly and handed Johan his mount's reins. Mounting quickly, Johan turned his horse and urged it swiftly down the trail, Rugal close behind. Treble, sensing something was wrong, remained hidden in Rugal's tunic as the two youths spurred their horses through the thick underbrush, heedless of the multitude of scratches each soon had on arms and legs as they scraped through brush and trees with single-minded purpose.

The trees were finally beginning to thin when Tag, Rugal's faithful bay, stumbled, moving with a violent limp for a few paces. Rugal almost tumbled from the saddle and pulled up on the reins, shouting to Johan to stop. Rugal quickly dismounted and picked up his horse's foreleg. Tag turned his head and regarded his master as Rugal lifted the horse's hoof and pulled a short dagger from his boot. Scraping the inside of the hoof, he found a large sharp stone lodged inside. Using his dagger, he worked it out and silently held it up to Johan.

Gently lowering the leg, he patted Tag's sweaty neck. "This stone must have caught in his hoof miles ago," he said sadly. "Tag is a valiant steed. He carried me a long way without complaint when he must have been suffering terribly."

Johan eyed Tag appreciatively. "He is indeed a fine horse." He didn't say anymore, waiting for Rugal to make the decision they both knew he must make.

Rugal wiped his hand tiredly across his forehead. He patted Tag again, murmuring to the horse, who rubbed his head against Rugal's shoulder in affection. "I'm sorry, Tag. But we must leave you behind," Rugal said softly. The big horse perked his ears at Rugal's voice as if he understood. Rugal slowly began to unsaddle Tag and directed his attention to Johan, who was sitting quietly on his sturdy mount.

"Tag obviously can't bear any weight." Rugal blew out a frustrated breath. "I can see no other solution except to turn him loose." He gazed at his favorite horse wistfully. "Hopefully, after we find Tonar, I can return for him. He'll probably head toward Laran, along with Tonar's mare."

He sighed and stroked Tag's neck one last time, then placed his saddle in some bushes, covering it with scattered branches. He handed his pack to Johan, who secured it next to his own. Johan nodded sympathetically and held his hand out. There was no help for it. They would have to ride double. Rugal paused, weighing the advantage of taking on an animal form that could accompany Johan with the Tolan youth's likely response. His *dynamis* gift was so rare, it startled even members of the Sepharim.

Making a quick decision, he grabbed Johan's hand and swung up behind him. Johan turned his horse, and when Tag started after them, Rugal forced himself to wave his arms and shout so that the horse would not follow. Tag finally stopped and lowered his head to graze. Relieved, Rugal gripped Johan's shoulders. "We can move more quickly now," he said regretfully. "Tag is no longer trying to keep up with us."

Johan, trying to be positive, replied, "Don't worry. Tag is a tough animal. I will return with you after we rescue Tonar, and we will find him, enjoying his vacation, no doubt."

Not waiting for a response, Johan urged his horse forward, and they continued northwest in an urgent silence, fear for Tonar's life outweighing all other thoughts.

CHAPTER NINE

True riches cannot be touched.
~ Nomadic Proverb

Dusk was approaching when they finally broke through the forest and onto a plain that extended towards a mountain range. Johan abruptly pulled up. The sun cast a rainbow of colors as it began its homeward journey, but neither youth had a mind to appreciate it.

"We better stop here," Johan said. "Raksh must rest. He's strong but unused to carrying two. And we must also rest and eat."

Rugal would much rather continue but knew Johan was being realistic and agreed. They dismounted, and Rugal gathered wood while Johan rubbed down his horse. He hobbled Raksh and set him loose to graze. It was dark when Johan seated himself by the fire Rugal had built. Feeling tired and dirty, with no stream nearby, the exhausted young men ate a sparse meal of dried meat and bread from their packs. Treble accepted some breadcrumbs from Johan's hand, then flew into a nearby tree and tucked his head under his wing. The stars crept out, illuminating the sky with their bright points of light.

Johan looked toward a particularly bright blue star that hovered near the horizon. Rugal followed his gaze, and Johan began to speak. "That star is of special significance to my people," he said softly. "It is a star of hope. Some of my people believe that Vellaquar carried the stone of fire from that star."

Rugal, exhausted from the journey and the day's frustrations, spoke sarcastically, more sharply than he intended. "Let's hope this Vellaquar of yours can guide us to Tonar; otherwise, I'm afraid I have little use for it."

Johan jerked back as if stung, and Rugal instantly regretted his words. He realized he had just insulted a man who could be a good friend, whom he had already grown to respect. He quickly apologized.

"I'm sorry, Johan. I'm tired and worried about Tonar. I did not mean those words and meant no insult to you."

Johan regarded Rugal intently, then relaxed. "My people have another belief," he said quietly. "Only a real man will admit when he is wrong." He smiled at Rugal. "Come, my friend," he said. "I think we'll both be able to think better after a good night's sleep."

Rugal grinned back, relieved that he had not alienated Johan with his words. Johan's diplomacy also made Rugal wonder. The thought that Johan was more than a simple messenger entered his mind again as they lay rolled in their blankets under the stars. He quickly wove a thread of protection for the night, and before he could dwell further on Johan's identity, sleep claimed him.

Johan's mount, gently whiffling at Johan, roused both young men from a deep sleep. Raksh shook his head restlessly, impatient to continue. The morning sun had barely risen, and the moon was still visible. Johan and Rugal ate a quick breakfast from their packs and, feeling rested, mounted on Johan's faithful horse and continued their journey. Both young men felt better and were eager to reach a village so they could get another mount and search for Tonar.

"There's a village about a quarter of a day's journey south," Johan commented.

"That must be Kepath," Rugal agreed. "I am sure I can locate some members of the Sepharim there. They will help us, and then we can search for Tonar." Rugal paused. He cleared his throat. "Do you think Tonar is alive?" he asked tentatively.

Johan nodded his head, trying to crane his neck back, but Raksh's forward motion prevented him from meeting Rugal's eyes. "Absolutely," he said firmly. "Either they think he is you and will need him alive for the Day of Questioning, or they know he is a member of your court and will use him for bait to try to lure you to them. Either way, it is in their best interests to keep him alive."

Rugal breathed a sigh of relief. "Yes, that makes sense. Thanks, Johan."

THE TWO RODE IN SILENCE, Johan concentrating on the road ahead and Rugal lost in thought. Treble, sensing Rugal's mood, stayed tucked in his tunic and slept. Skirting the forest, the open plain left them feeling vulnerable, and they wanted to get to Kepath as soon as they could. Finally, the outskirts of a small settlement came into view. Rather than stop for lunch, they decided to forge ahead and soon found themselves on a cleared path leading to the customary watch tower, a relic from

Oldag's reign of terror. Unlike Laran, no one rode out to meet them on the path, but a youth a few years younger than Rugal approached them on foot, curiosity written all over the towheaded boy's face.

Johan pulled Raksh to a halt a few feet away from the youth. "Greetings and welcome to Kepath," the lad gave a quick bow, his sharp eyes taking in their disheveled appearance. "My name is Dendin." It was obvious that Dendin was bursting to ask what had caused them to ride double on what was obviously an onerous journey, but he held his tongue, waiting for the travelers to speak.

Raksh moved restlessly, and Johan soothed him, rubbing his neck as he waited for Rugal to take the lead. Unfamiliar with the customs of Elayas, he didn't want to arouse suspicion.

Rugal leaned around Johan and smiled down at Dendin. "Thank you for the welcome, Dendin. I am Yandin, and this is Jolan, my cousin. We have been traveling to visit relatives in Farath, having been granted a brief respite from our apprenticeship in Cargoa. Unfortunately, my horse spooked at a wolf in the woods, and I was caught off-guard. We are horse trainers, and I was using the trip as an opportunity to put some training miles on him. He threw me and took off." He shrugged his shoulders. "So here we are. Could you please direct us to any lodging that is available in Kepath? We will need to purchase another horse in order to continue our journey and get a good night's rest."

Dendin pursed his lips, thinking about where to direct them, when he noticed Treble peeking out of Rugal's tunic. Curious, he stepped closer, and his eyes widened.

"Aye–it's a flutebird! I know because my uncle has one. How did you come by it?" he exclaimed.

Rugal fought down the panic he felt at their identities being revealed and managed a calm smile. "Why, is that what he is? I was wondering that. I found him in the woods all tuckered out before I got thrown from my horse. I dug up some worms and fed him, and he has decided to stay with me since."

Dendin nodded, his eyes glowing as he looked at Treble. He seemed satisfied with Rugal's explanation and turned back to the problem at hand. "There is a room available at the tavern for rent." He pointed toward the main road that went by the tower. "Just follow that road and when you get to the cross-section, the tavern will be on the right-hand corner."

"Thank you, Dendin." Johan reached down to clasp the boy's hand.

Much to their surprise, Dendin hastily stepped back. He looked away and muttered, "Glad to help."

Johan frowned, withdrawing his hand. Rugal cleared his throat, drawing Dendin's gaze to him. "We appreciate the information, Dendin. Good day to you." He gave Johan a nudge, and Raksh started down the road Dendin had indicated. When they were out of the boy's earshot, Rugal squeezed Johan's shoulder. "I'm sorry. I was very encouraged in Laran, but it seems there are still some pockets of prejudice toward Tolan. I have been made aware that our citizens sometimes identify anyone from Tolan with Oldag, since it is well-known that he was born there. The Tolan people have distinctly different physical characteristics that are readily identifiable." Rugal attempted a joke. "Although it worked to your advantage at the dance."

Johan smiled briefly at the memory, then sighed. "I was afraid that might be the case. People often struggle with the idea of interacting with those different from themselves. It seems to be a universal problem. In fact, I thought it would be an obstacle in convincing you to join me."

"It was," Rugal admitted. "But I am very glad I was able to set aside my own prejudice. I would have lost the opportunity of getting to know you." He paused, brushing his hair back from his forehead. "And the opportunity of making a friend."

"Thanks, Rugal. The feeling is mutual."

The two rode in silence, passing shops and houses and the occasional passerby on horse or foot as they traversed the main road. The townspeople stared at the strangers on horseback, but no one stopped to engage them. Reaching the intersection Dendin had described, Rugal drew a sigh of relief. The old but well-kept building had an area off to the side with a filled water trough and a place to tie horses while they waited for the patrons inside. The grass had been eaten down to the nubs, but a sign on a stack of hay indicated it was for sale and to pay inside.

Rugal and Johan slid down from Raksh, and Johan led Raksh over for a drink, then tied him to one of the posts, leaving the dun-colored horse munching on the hay Rugal brought over from the stack. Treble flew onto a branch in a nearby tree and started preening his feathers. The two young men entered the tavern and glanced around the room. Rough-hewn wooden tables were scattered about, and as most taverns were, the light was dim, with only an occasional candle in a sconce on the wall to provide illumination. Lunchtime had already passed, and the tavern had emptied as its patrons returned to their various occupations. The two were hungry and chose a table toward the back so they could order a meal. Rugal walked up to the barkeeper and smiled.

"Greetings. We are tired and hungry, having just come through the forest between here and Laran." He gazed at the short man in an apron on the other side of the counter. "My cousin and I would like some lunch, and we'll also need to pay for the hay our horse is eating."

"Certainly," the barkeeper replied, wiping his hands on a

dish towel. "If you want to sit down, I'll bring your meal to you."

Rugal sat across from Johan, and neither spoke, digging with enthusiasm into the roast beef and potatoes the barkeeper had placed on their table. Finally feeling full, they sat back, sipping their ales.

"I guess we should see about renting a room," Rugal wiped the sleeve of his tunic across his mouth. While the journey had been tiring, he was enjoying getting to dispense with maintaining the courtly appearance expected of a king.

"Good idea," Johan agreed.

Rugal lowered his voice. "I need to locate a member of the Sepharim. We are going to need their help in obtaining another horse."

Johan rubbed his cheek. "How will we do that without revealing our identities? As you already noticed, Dendin was not overly friendly, and we got some strange looks on our way in. I am not sure of our welcome."

"I got the same feeling. I think it best..."

Rugal stopped talking as a man of average height with brown hair approached their table. He had entered a few minutes before and sat at the bar with a mug of ale. Now that they had finished their meal, holding his mug, he made his way over and smiled at the pair. Rugal raised his eyebrows as he pulled up a chair. Before he could say anything, the man put his mug on the table and, directing his gaze at Rugal, asked in a pleasant tone, "Have you an interest in music?"

Rugal jerked back in surprise, then gathered his composure. He met the man's eyes squarely. "We hope to see Stargazer soon."

The man smiled, "Good Afternoon, Sire," he said in a low voice. "My name is Nirkut."

Seeing the look of confusion on Johan's face, Rugal turned

to him and explained, "Legas gave me the code before we left. Our friend here is a member of the Sepharim and can be trusted." Rugal silently thanked the Swordsman for his foresight. He turned back to the man. "But how did you know?"

The man laughed. "News of a flutebird travels fast," he grinned. "Dendin has told everyone about yours. But don't worry–he believed your story. He is actually hoping that your flutebird decides to stay here in Kepath." He turned serious. "But what happened? I was told there would be three of you on horseback." He raised his eyebrows. "All I see is one horse and the two of you."

Rugal rubbed the back of his neck. "It's a long story, and we need your help. Why don't I go rent a room? We'll meet there, where we can talk more privately."

"Good idea, Sire. There is only one room, and it is around the back with an outside entry. I know the tavern owner–he is a Patriotes. I'll make the necessary arrangements for you and meet you there in an hour." He paused and studied Johan for a long moment. "I hope you are holding up, Johan. We are not the friendliest town to strangers, and Oldag's legacy has a long reach."

"Thank you, Nirkut. It hasn't been exactly pleasant, but I know Rugal has my back."

"Then you are a rich man indeed," Nirkut got up and, with a wink, headed out the door.

CHAPTER TEN

To ride a good horse is to feel the winds of heaven.
~ Mergolith Proverb

Tonar lay on the ground, his hands tied in front of him, as his captors walked about the meadow in what appeared to be a heated argument. He couldn't understand their language, but it was obvious the two men who had grabbed him from his horse had a disagreement. He occasionally caught a word he understood. Rugal and Elayas were mentioned, along with Tolan and Kargolith. He closed his eyes briefly in frustration, but quickly opened them. He felt far from safe and thought it best to keep his captors in sight.

The hours since his capture were a blur. Tonar remembered fighting with one of the men and had a torn tunic to prove it. They had managed to hold him down and tie his hands. He continued to struggle but soon realized it was doing no good and only expended his energy, so he stopped and became compliant, following the lead man while the other trotted behind them. They had moved at a jog for several hours, eating nuts and berries and sipping water from a leather flask. He had spent the night miserably, huddled in a blanket between his captors. At the first streaks of daylight, they had roughly helped him to his feet, and they continued their journey. Tonar had no idea where they were headed.

Both men were stocky, with black hair and dark complexions. They wore clothes that looked similar to what Tonar was used to seeing, with the exception that their tunics were longer and had a pattern stitched around the cuffs and bottom hem. The taller of the two approached and gazed down at him.

"Good morning, King Rugal," the man's words were heavily accented, and Tonar had to strain to understand him. "We are sorry for the taking, but we must have you with us."

Tonar could tell the man was struggling to find the right words in a language not his own, but the meaning was clear. They thought he was Rugal, and they had a purpose for kidnapping him. He gazed up at his captor, thinking about what to say. He could keep these men from pursuing Rugal if he pretended that they were correct. By keeping up the pretense, he could give Rugal and Johan time to reach their destination.

Tonar glared at his captor. "And this is how you would treat a king?" he demanded in his most regal voice. He looked down at his hands that were tied.

"Our apologies, Sire," the man gazed back earnestly. "We have no choice. We need your help."

Tonar raised his eyebrows indignantly. "You have a funny way of asking for it. Here in Elayas, we request help. We don't force people against their will."

The man cleared his throat and looked away, then back at

Tonar. "We do what we have to. Since you are friends with Tolan, you would not have considered our request."

Tonar, remembering the conversation in the library, blurted out, "You have the ring."

The man jerked his head back and shook it. "I don't. But we are going to where it is being held."

Tonar's eyes narrowed. "Where is that? And you know who I am, but you haven't introduced yourself."

The man glanced over at his companion nervously and licked his lips. "Let us just say we are an interested party in what happens at the Tolan border."

"That's not good enough," Tonar pushed to his knees, then awkwardly stood, drawing himself up to his full height. "You owe me an explanation for this rough treatment. Even now, my friends are surely coming after you. Why would you steal the ring and then risk kidnapping the king?"

The man looked down. "I am sorry, King Rugal, but you will have to wait until we arrive at our destination." He reached down and tested the ropes encircling Tonar's wrists, loosening them a tiny bit. "This should make you more comfortable." He held his water flask to Tonar's lips, and Tonar took a couple of gulps and accepted the dried meat the man offered to him, holding it between his palms and munching on it. The man's companion barked out some words.

"We must keep moving. You can eat while we walk." With that, he propelled Tonar in the direction he wanted him to go, and the three set off at a fast pace through the woods.

RUGAL AND JOHAN lingered over their drinks. Johan shook his

head in amazement. "Your Tamadar is very well connected. It is making our journey much easier."

Rugal nodded. "If only it had extended to those cursed kidnappers. We need to find Tonar, and fast."

"Yes, Sire, but first, we need to get another horse. My Raksh is gallant, but carrying two is wearing on him."

"Yes, of course," he blew out a noisy breath. "My guess is that Nirkut is already working on that. We'd best get to the room and figure out our next steps."

"Of course, Sire," Johan agreed in a low voice. The two stood up, and Rugal made his way back to the bar. He gave the barkeeper a silver piece to cover their lunch and Raksh's hay. The two young men headed out the front door, and Johan checked on Raksh; the sturdy gelding's head was lowered, and he was dozing under the shade of a tree, having eaten the hay Rugal had given him. His rear leg was cocked in a relaxed position, his only movement an occasional swish of his tail. Treble, spotting Rugal, flew down from the tree and landed on his shoulder. Following Nirkut's instructions, they went around the building toward the outside entrance of the room in back. As they quickly rounded the corner, they startled a big red horse that was at the end of a lead rope being held by Nirkut, and the horse spooked in place, ears perked forward.

"Now that's a good horse," Johan commented, gazing at the muscular gelding with admiration. "He didn't jump off to the side like most horses would."

"That's exactly right, Johan," Nirkut agreed. "He is from the stables of a local Patriotes that raises fine horses. His name is Flash."

"Flash," Rugal murmured, holding out his hand so the big horse could smell him. "Ahhhh...Tag would be jealous. But I think he would understand."

The big horse shook his head and blew out from his

nostrils, as if in agreement. Rugal turned to Nirkut. "Thank you. He is a fine mount."

"Fit for a king," Nirkut grinned. "Come, let's get both your mounts to the stables and then come back here to plan out the best strategy for your venture."

TREBLE PERCHED on the back of Rugal's chair as Rugal, Johan, and Nirkut sat around the table in the sparsely furnished room. Rugal explained what had happened in the woods, and Nirkut leaned back, sympathy in his eyes as he considered the situation. "I'm sorry your friend has been captured. Since you didn't see his captors, we can't even be sure who they are. And why Tonar? Why not Rugal?" His eyes narrowed. "Unless they mistook Tonar for Rugal."

"That is what we think," Rugal rubbed his neck tiredly. "And we don't know if they have discovered their mistake yet. Knowing Tonar, he'll play along in order to protect me. But if they put the Ring of Rosin on him, they'll know he's not the king of Elayas."

Johan cleared his throat, drawing Nirkut's attention. "I rode to the castle with the message that we were certain some Kargoliths were traveling to Cargoa in an attempt to kidnap King Rugal. I think Tonar's captors must be the men I came to warn King Rugal about. Their ability to approach us stealthily is a skill their nomadic lifestyle requires."

Drumming his fingers on the table, Nirkut looked from Rugal to Johan and back to Rugal again. "I know you want to save your friend, but I think the best thing you can do is continue your journey."

Rugal half stood out of his chair in protest, but Nirkut

raised a hand. "Hear me out, Sire." His unwavering gaze brought Rugal back into his seat. "If they are the Kargoliths, which is most likely, they are masters at blending into the landscape, and they are probably well on their way to their destination. I think the best thing you can do for Tonar and for Elayas is to keep going."

Standing up, Johan walked over to Rugal and put a hand on his shoulder. "Nirkut's right. I want to try to find Tonar too, but it would be impossible to determine which direction they have gone. Our best chance to help him is to get to the Kargolith camp in time to enter their sacred court and demand the Rite of Reciprocity."

Rugal stared down at the table, rubbing the edge with a finger. He thought he would never again feel like he had when the guardsman had attacked Felan while he was defending a poor old man, and Rugal couldn't stop the guardsman from killing his beloved teacher. He hated feeling helpless, and every fiber of his being wanted to take action. But he knew Nirkut and Johan were right. Even if he turned into a bear or a wolf–he had no idea which direction to go. He nodded his head slowly. "You're right, of course." He looked up at Johan. "It's nearly nightfall. We won't be able to leave until tomorrow. I guess the best thing we can do is get some rest and start fresh early in the morning."

Johan signaled his agreement, and Nirkut stood up. "I think that is most wise, Sire. You will find Flash a willing mount, and I daresay, with an early start, you will feel refreshed and make good time. Dinner will be served at the tavern in an hour, and your room and meal are already paid for. Try to get some rest. You'll do Tonar the most good by being fit of both mind and body when you enter the Kargolith's domain."

"Thank you, Nirkut. That sounds like a good plan."

"Then, if you don't require anything further..." Nirkut's voice trailed off.

"You have been more than helpful, Nirkut. Just one more thing."

"Yes, Sire?"

"Can you explain the lack of welcome we have received here? It is a much different reception than we received in Laran."

Nirkut sighed. "Yes, Sire. Kepath is much closer to Tolan." He hesitated, glancing at Johan with discomfiture. "The townspeople of Kepath don't really care for the Tolan people or the Kargoliths who occasionally travel through or come to trade here."

Johan's head jerked up. "Why is that?" he asked, his eyes glittering.

Nirkut blew out a noisy breath. "I think people are just naturally afraid of anyone different than themselves. It's not a fair way of thinking, but that's just how most people are."

Rugal nodded thoughtfully. "You make a good point. Most people are uncomfortable when having to do something unfamiliar. That would extend to interacting with unfamiliar people." He smiled at the man who had provided so much assistance. "Thank you, Nirkut." He briefly inclined his head. "I appreciate your service."

"Thank you, Sire," the man gave a half bow. "It has been a pleasure." He turned to Johan. "It has been a pleasure to meet you as well. Good fortune on your journey."

CHAPTER ELEVEN

"Be yourself–No one else can. You are unique, and the world needs you."
~ Felan, Master of the Sepharim

"Mura! Jackal!" Lissa screamed, her face flushed with fear. She was in the front courtyard sitting on the bench she and Rugal often dallied at, when Tag and Tonar's horse came trotting through the trees. Fear for Rugal gripped Lissa, weighing her down, and she felt a stone in the pit of her stomach.

Mura and Jackal, along with the castle staff, came running. When Mura saw Tag riderless, she came to an abrupt halt, putting her hand to her throat. Jackal continued to Lissa, who had stood up, her face white as a sheet. He gently held her arm and helped her sit back down.

"What do you think happened?" Lissa's voice was shaking.

Jackal didn't say what he was thinking–that it was Rugal's

and Tonar's horses in the courtyard but not Johan's. *Could Johan have attacked them? Were they foolish to trust someone they knew so little about?* He shook his head and turned his attention back to Lissa, who sat clenching the sides of the bench, her eyes squeezed shut. He could hear her whisper and leaned in to listen.

"Are you sure? Yes, I will. When? I love you, too." She sat up and opened her eyes. Her face was drawn with exhaustion, but also relief. "He's okay," she whispered, then fell forward, Jackal barely catching her in time before she hit the grass, unconscious.

THE SWORDSMAN STRODE into the room where Jackal had carried Lissa and placed her carefully on a couch. Mura covered her with a blanket and when she started to stir, Mura brought her a cup of steaming tea. Lissa wrapped her hands around the mug, color finally returning to her face. Mura leaned forward anxiously, and Lissa offered her a small smile. "I was able to talk with Rugal, Mura. He is okay. Tag came up lame in the middle of a forest, so he had to turn him loose. Rugal is with Johan."

"That makes sense," Jackal agreed. "Tag was limping slightly when Yandin caught him. But what of Tonar's mount?"

Lissa's expression turned to dismay. "Someone has kidnapped Tonar. They don't know who, but they believe his captors have mistaken him for Rugal and are taking him to the Kargolith encampment for the Day of Questioning." She wiped a tear that had started to trickle down her cheek. "Johan has advised Rugal that they continue their journey, since they have no way to find Tonar. Their hope is that they will find him when they find the Kargoliths and will be able to rescue him."

"How will Rugal travel?" the Swordsman asked, his huge frame tense.

"You have done well, Swordsman," Lissa replied, smiling gently at the big man who was obviously worried for Rugal's safety. "Members of the Sepharim have come to their aid. He and Johan are leaving in the morning. Rugal will be mounted on a borrowed steed provided by Nirkut."

The Swordsman let out a breath of relief, and the tension in his shoulders eased. "Nirkut is a good man." He gazed at Lissa curiously. "How do you know all this?"

Lissa looked down, considering his question. She took a sip of tea. "I'm not sure what triggered it." She smiled, her eyes glowing. "But I can communicate with Rugal." She paused, remembering the day Rugal had confronted Oldag. "I remember that I had felt drawn to Rugal the first time I saw him. I could feel his thoughts, and I had to hold my *dynamis* in check, so I did not influence the battle. I knew he had to fight in his own strength. Rugal had to believe in himself. But this is different..." her voice trailed off, as she struggled to understand what had happened.

The Swordsman pulled a chair over and lightly put his hand on her arm. "You knew you had *dynamis*, but you never understood your specific potential–is that right?" he asked calmly.

Lissa met his gaze. "That's right, Swordsman. My father recognized the gift in me, but we have been waiting for it to reveal itself."

"Well, now we know," The Swordsman's face split into a grin. "It's fairly rare, like Rugal's, but we know what it is." He turned to Mura and Jackal. "It is fitting for Ethiod's daughter and our future queen to have such a fine gift." He turned back to Lissa. "You are Ethiod's legacy. I think Rugal will be pleased."

Lissa jerked back, eyes wide. "So, can I communicate with everyone that way?" her voice quavered.

"We don't know enough about it yet," the Swordsman replied. "The extent of who you can communicate with is unknown–it will be revealed as you use it. But don't worry," he gently patted her shoulder reassuringly. "We will help you master it. You are a member of the Sepharim, after all."

RUGAL AND JOHAN returned to their room after a simple but hot meal of meat, bread, and cheese in the tavern. No one had approached their table. They ate quickly in peace, then headed back to the small room, each taking a chair. The evening chorus of insects and frogs began serenading them. A comfortable silence fell between the two companions until suddenly, Rugal, obviously not addressing Johan, started speaking in a low voice. Johan looked at Rugal curiously.

"What was that all about?"

"What do you mean?" Rugal responded nonchalantly.

"You were talking to yourself."

Rugal cocked an eyebrow at Johan. "I wasn't talking to myself," he replied firmly.

Johan gave him a sideways look. "Whatever you say. That's what it looked like."

Rugal grinned. "Actually, I was talking to Lissa."

Johan raised both his eyebrows. "Now, how could that be possible? She is back at the castle."

Unable to contain himself any longer, Rugal jumped up, eyes

shining. "We just found out Lissa's gift. Tag and Tonar's horse came into the castle courtyard, scaring Lissa and triggering her ability to communicate across great distances. She can talk to me!"

"What do you mean?" Johan asked, the hairs on the back of his neck lifting.

"I could hear her voice in my head. She told me about the horses and wanted to know if we were okay."

Johan stared at his companion, a mixture of fear, concern, and disbelief warring for expression. He leaned back in his chair. His hand trembled slightly as he considered Rugal's words. "You are strange folk indeed," he whispered. "Can she know what you are thinking?"

Rugal sensed Johan was unsure of how to respond to his revelation about Lissa's ability. He reminded himself that *dynamis* was not a part of Tolan culture–one of the reasons Oldag's parents had emigrated to Elayas. The gifts were almost unheard of where Johan was from. People were often afraid of the unfamiliar. "It's okay, Johan. Lissa can't know what anyone is thinking. It is like having a conversation, except in our heads. It is also very draining for her, although I didn't feel anything unusual afterward." He paused. "Hmmm... I don't even know if she can talk to anyone else. That's part of learning about your gift–it is a process of finding out the full extent of what you can do."

Taking a calming breath, Johan nodded. "Sorry, Rugal. I really enjoyed the life force ceremony you shared the other day, but this is all very new. The thought of someone in my head is, well...disconcerting, to say the least."

Rugal nodded reassuringly. "I know how you feel, Johan. The first time I experienced my own *dynamis*, it was quite a shock–and I was living at a Sepharim school." He gave Johan a light punch in the shoulder. "You'll get used to it, my friend. It is my hope that we are able to share each other's cultures–I think everyone will be better for it."

Johan's eyes glittered, and he rubbed the side of his nose. "I hope so, too." He turned and looked out the one window in the room. The stars were shining brightly in the night sky.

"I find it comforting to think that no matter where I am, I see the same stars that Lissa does." Rugal paused for a moment. "Just like you and your family also see the same stars."

Johan jerked back and looked at Rugal in surprise. Rugal returned his gaze, compassion shining in his eyes.

Johan gave a small smile. "Thank you, Sire. It is a very good thing to remember."

CHAPTER TWELVE

A stranger can be a friend, if given the chance.
~ Dalbenian Saying

"Looks like we are entering another forest," Rugal commented. They had left Kepath early, eager to be on their way. The fact that they had not received the warm welcome he expected during their time in Kepath stuck in Rugal's mind, something to reflect on once they were done with the business at hand. He held the reins lightly as Flash shook his head and danced in place, eager to move forward. Rugal felt a bit guilty. Flash was on the same level as Tag in being a responsive mount and just as powerful. He stroked the big red horse's neck and made a soothing noise.

"It's the Forest of Tarago," Johan looked around, eyes bright. "We are only a day away from our destination."

"Exactly where are we going?" Rugal rubbed his cheek.

Treble shifted his weight on Rugal's shoulder and hopped lightly to sit on the back of his saddle.

"If all goes well, we will be able to shelter in the woods near the Kargolith encampment," Johan looked pensive. "Hopefully, we will see Tonar there, and we can finalize our plans." A look of concern crossed his face, then disappeared. "The Day of Questioning is rapidly approaching. We need to keep going."

Rugal nodded in agreement. The thought that there was more to Johan than he had shared crossed his mind yet again, but he sensed now was not the right time to ask. He touched his heels to Flash's sides. Unlike the previous forest, this one had a well-worn trail, and they began to follow it, Rugal taking the lead. Flash and Raksh moved at a ground-eating trot, and soon, Kepath was far off in the distance as they traveled deeper into the forest. They ate dried meat and bread from their saddle bags, eager to cover as much ground as possible.

Rugal was chewing on a piece of meat when the path curved. Rounding the bend, Flash planted his feet, coming to a sudden stop, almost pitching Rugal over his head and causing Treble to fly up to the branch of a nearby tree. The red horse threw his head up and pinned his ears at the creature crouched in the path. A black wolf, its hackles raised, emitted a low growl and bared its teeth.

Why was the wolf holding its ground instead of running away? There had to be something holding him there. Instinct took over, and Rugal leapt to the ground, turning into a bear as soon as his feet landed on the forest floor. The transformation had become very familiar, and he no longer held out his hands to look at the furry paws terminating into sharp claws. With a roar, he sprang toward the wolf.

"Stop! Don't hurt him!"

Startled, Rugal allowed himself to fall short and came

down on all fours. He swung his massive head back and forth, looking for the source of the voice. Turning toward a tree, he saw a tall youth striding toward him. He had dark hair and appeared to be a little older than Rugal. Johan had jumped off Raksh and grabbed Flash's reins, trying to calm both horses, who did not like being near dangerous predators.

Rugal took a breath, and an instant later resumed human form. He stood on the path as the wolf ran to the youth and stayed at his side as he approached Rugal and came to a stop in front of him. His face was pale and his eyes wide, and he looked Rugal up and down. Finally, he blew out the breath he had been holding. He reached down and petted the wolf and met Rugal's gaze.

"I don't know how you did that, but thank you for not attacking the wolf. He is my friend."

Rugal arched an eyebrow. "It would be best if your friend did not crouch in the forest path–it is easy to mistake him for a wild animal ready to attack." He could feel Johan's gaze drilling into his back. His expression softened. "As for my changing into a bear, it is my *dynamis*. I am a member of the Sepharim."

He half-turned to Johan, and seeing the shock written on his face that Johan was trying to conceal, Rugal smiled apologetically. "It just never came up." He turned back to the youth.

"Who are you, and what business do you have roaming the forest?"

The young man met his gaze squarely. "I am called Zerdin. Our family has a farm on the edge of Elayas just past the Beren forest. I have been traveling with my friend to purchase seed for our farm."

"Greetings, Zerdin. I am Yandin, and this is my companion, Jolan." Rugal looked at the wolf, eyebrows raised. "How did you come to befriend a wolf?"

"I found him as an injured pup," Zerdin replied, stroking

the wolf's neck. The wolf gazed up toward Zerdin with obvious affection.

Rugal nodded, "I can understand that type of connection." He held up his hand, and Treble flew from his perch onto Rugal's shoulder. The flutebird chirped at the wolf, and the wolf wagged his tail slowly in return.

"It seems our creatures of the forest have agreed to be friends. I trust their instincts more than many people I have met. Shall we follow their example?" Rugal stretched out his hand.

Zerdin nodded and clasped it with his own. The horses had settled down and stood quietly, heads dropped as they took advantage of the opportunity to rest. Zerdin walked over to Johan and they also exchanged handshakes.

Rugal looked at the young man and came to a decision. "I see you aren't mounted, Zerdin. We can offer you a ride until we clear the forest. After that, we must proceed due south, but until then, Flash is big and strong. You can ride behind me." Rugal tilted his head. "Of course, the choice is yours."

"I appreciate the offer, Yandin. As long as my wolf friend can run alongside, I would be glad to take you up on it." Rugal took in the scene before him, noting that the horses had grown accustomed to the wolf's presence in even this short amount of time. It spoke to their superb training, which included following the cues of their master. Rugal and Johan were not upset at the presence of the wolf, so both equines trusted that there was no reason for them to be either.

"Everyone is getting along without fuss," Rugal glanced at Johan, who nodded. "I think that will be fine."

Johan strode forward and offered Flash's reins to Rugal, who gathered them in one hand, and grasped Flash's mane with the other. He leapt easily into the saddle, then offered his hand to Zerdin, who grasped it and just as easily sprang into place behind Rugal. Johan mounted Raksh and, taking the lead, headed down the clearly defined path. Treble positioned himself against Rugal's chest, and the wolf trotted easily through the forest, occasionally disappearing in the brush as he maintained a parallel path to the two equines.

"Are you hungry?" Rugal asked Zerdin as they made their way at a good pace through the forest.

"I am," Zerdin admitted hesitantly. "But I have no wish to impose beyond what I am already. Flash is an amazing steed–he has the smoothest pace I have ever ridden."

Rugal glanced over his shoulder at Zerdin, grinning. "Indeed, he does. But you are not imposing. When someone is hungry, and another has food, we must share our sustenance. Caring for one another is the right thing to do." He patted the saddle bag. "Reach in there and grab some dried meat and bread."

The youth did as Rugal instructed and ate a simple meal as they rode.

After allowing Zerdin enough time to finish eating, Rugal inquired politely, "From whom will you be buying your seed? Can your family not afford a horse to take you to your destination?"

Zerdin stiffened a bit in the saddle, then relaxed. "I'm sorry, Yandin. It is a sore point with me. My favorite stallion is being used to plow our fields. If I didn't leave him behind, we would not have the fields ready in time for the fall planting." He sighed. "We purchase our seeds from a master cultivator. He lives in the territory between Elayas and Tolan. It's quite a journey on foot, but my wolf friend accompanies me."

"I understand," Rugal grinned. "Sometimes, my duties do not allow me time to ride either."

"Your duties?" Zerdin asked. "You're apprenticed then?"

"Yes," Rugal replied easily. "I am apprenticed to be a blacksmith." Rugal was thankful his sword practice with the Sword of Fate had given him the muscular arms of a smith–it was a good cover story.

Zerdin nodded. "A most excellent trade. May you experience much success."

"Thank you, Zerdin. And may your crops burst from your fields in abundance."

THE SUN WAS WELL on its downward trek when they finally broke through the forest. An occasional tree dotted the grassland ahead.

"Ah, here we are," Johan pulled up Raksh, who lowered his head, panting slightly from the day's exertions. Flash stopped before running into Raksh, and Johan looked pointedly at Rugal. "It looks like we are at the place where our paths must part."

Rugal reluctantly nodded. They had to find Tonar and figure out a way to rescue him. Having Zerdin along would complicate matters. "It seems so."

Zerdin took their cue and slid from Flash's back, allowing his legs to readjust to being on the ground. Rugal reached into his saddle bag and handed the young man some dried bread and meat. "I know you have your wolf friend to watch out for you, but having some extra food for your journey won't hurt and will save you some time."

Zerdin accepted the food with a grateful expression and reached his arm up to clasp Rugal's. His wolf friend suddenly appeared and gazed intently at Rugal, his yellow eyes unreadable but his sharp teeth visible in a canine grin. He slowly wagged his tail and whined. Flash broke the moment by jigging to one side, more out of habit than fear. Prey animals instinctively avoid predators and after a long day of being ridden double, he had reached his limit.

Zerdin turned and walked to Johan and clasped his arm as well. He smiled at both of them. "Your kindness won't be forgotten. Thank you." And with that, he turned and started striding northwest, his wolf companion trotting by his side.

CHAPTER
THIRTEEN

"The greater the power–the greater the duty."
~ King Rugal

Rugal and Johan spent an uneasy night under the shelter of a tree and then rapidly made their way across the gently rolling terrain, until a small body of water in the distance came into view.

"I think we are close," Johan commented. "See that lake? Being nomadic, the Kargoliths would camp close to a water source. That lake is the only one in this region. I think their encampment must be there."

"Is that where the sacred court is held?"

"Yes, and also where they would be holding Tonar. The Kargoliths have semi-permanent encampments throughout the unsettled territory according to the seasons."

Rugal raised his eyebrows. "How do you know so much about them?"

Johan smiled. "The King of Tolan has his people out in the field. This is common knowledge for those in his service. The Kargoliths have presented a threat to Tolan for many years."

Rugal nodded, deciding not to press Johan further. They needed to focus on the task in front of them. They dismounted near a stand of trees and hobbled Flash and Raksh far enough back from where Johan thought the encampment was located to remain undetected. Both horses began happily munching grass while their masters scouted the area.

Rugal and Johan were hoping to locate where Tonar was being kept before nightfall. The coming darkness would make it more difficult to determine his whereabouts. About a quarter mile from the horses, they lay on their bellies, peering through the fringe of trees that bordered the Kargolith encampment.

"Are you sure Tonar is there?" Rugal whispered.

Johan's eyes glittered. "Yes, he has to be there. From what we know of the Kargoliths, this encampment is where their leaders gather, and decisions are made. His captors would have brought him there for safekeeping."

Rugal gave Johan a sidelong glance, but Johan easily returned his look with a grim smile. "The King of Tolan has his agents, just like the Tamadar has his. We have studied their movements and have an accurate picture of the patterns they follow as they move about. If they thought they had captured you, they would have brought you to this encampment."

Before Rugal could question Johan further, both young men swiveled their heads toward the sound of a scuffle to their left. Tonar came into view, his arms bound in front of him, with a man on either side. Tonar was not making their job easy, as he tried to dodge into the direction of the woods, and the two men had to restrain him. Rugal was relieved to see they did not harm him as they did so. They must still believe Tonar was Rugal and needed him to be in good health for the Day of Questioning.

Rugal's eyes remained locked on Tonar. "He looks to be unharmed. We need to rescue him before anything happens to him."

Johan tilted his head, taking in the layout of the encampment. "They would be foolish to harm him. They need him to cooperate when it comes to asking the Ring of Rosin their questions." His eyes grew serious. "The new moon is tonight. If we are going to have a chance for you to demand the Right of Reciprocity, we need to get you to the sacred circle so that you can reveal your identity and demand the return of the Ring of Rosin. The Kargolith tribal elders will be duty-bound to do so, and to release Tonar at your behest."

Johan pointed at a tall, muscular man a few yards from where Tonar was sitting between his guards, holding a piece of dried meat between his bound hands, nibbling on it. "Do you see that man across from Tonar? The one with a pouch around his neck?"

Rugal nodded. "Yes, he reminds me of the Swordsman–someone you would not lightly challenge to a duel."

"You are correct," Johan responded. "He is a fierce warrior called Dungellan. He must have been given the task of guarding the Ring of Rosin until it is needed for the Day of Questioning. The ring is most likely in the pouch around his neck."

Rugal closed his eyes tightly, reaching out with his *dynamis*. He jerked back as a flash of recognition passed between him and the contents of the pouch. He opened his eyes and noted Dungellan looking down at the pouch with a puzzled expression. Finally, the big man shrugged, apparently choosing to disregard whatever he thought he might have felt.

"The Ring of Rosin is definitely in the pouch," Rugal agreed.

"I made a brief connection with it using my *dynamis.*" Rugal watched the big man wearing the pouch for a few moments. "Dungellan looks like an excellent choice for the task," Rugal observed. He sighed. "This will not be easy."

As Rugal lay on the ground observing the Kargoliths, the press of the grass against his body and its green, earthy smell reminded him of another time he lay in the grass–the day he had discovered his *dynamis*. After turning into a bear, his beloved teacher, Felan, had found him lying in the grass after his headlong run that ended in his turning back into a boy. The old desire to run started to rise within him, but he recognized it for what it was–something that no longer had a hold on him. He effortlessly shoved the feeling aside and smiled. "Yes, Felan–I'm not running anymore," he whispered to himself.

"We better stay here until it gets dark. Can you use your *dynamis* to change into a bear again?"

Johan's query jerked Rugal out of his reverie.

"Yes, I can." He looked at Johan with a mischievous smile tugging at the corners of his mouth. "Or any other animal I choose."

Johan's eyes widened, and he let out a gasp. "Any animal? That must be amazing!"

"It is," Rugal admitted, his expression turning serious. "But the obligation that comes with it can be quite heavy. The greater the power–the greater the duty."

Johan's eyes took on a reflective look, and his shoulders stiffened. "I can see how that would be so." He shook his head to clear it. "We had better plan what to do, once it gets dark. The new moon represents new beginnings and a time of planning for the month ahead. The tribal elders will be gathered in the sacred court."

He paused, rubbing his chin. "The new moon will not be visible, so only the sacred fire will provide illumination. We should be able to get fairly close to the sacred circle." He glanced back at Rugal. "You can't use your *dynamis* to enter it. We can't give them any reason to withhold the Rite of Reciprocity."

"What do you mean? What would that have to do with anything?"

"You must remember, *dynamis* is rare in Tolan, and I think it is unheard of in the Kargolith tribe. You don't want to do anything that would cause them to refuse your claim. Better to keep your ability a secret, at least for now."

Johan obviously had much more experience with the Kargoliths, and a wise king listened to the counsel of those with more experience than he. Rugal's eyebrows crinkled. "Could you please elaborate on the Kargoliths and the sacred court? They are very different from anyone I have ever encountered."

"Of course," Johan assented. "So, the elders of the tribe will be seated closest to the platform. The Kargoliths further back are the tribespeople gathered to witness the monthly ceremony of the sacred court, which is when decisions are made that impact the entire tribe."

Johan paused, shifting to a more comfortable position. "The Kargoliths are nomadic and move to different encampments throughout the year. Those present today are only a fraction of the tribe, which is believed to number around two thousand. The other Kargoliths are scattered at different camps, but maintain an attachment to the main encampment, which is here. Representatives are sent each month to be present at the sacred court."

Rugal rubbed his chin thoughtfully, taking it all in. He gazed intently at Johan. "Okay, I understand, thanks. So, what's the plan?"

Johan drew a breath and blew it out. "Here is what I think will have the strongest possibility for success..."

CHAPTER
FOURTEEN

Don't fight the wrong enemy.
~ Ancient Proverb (Unknown Origin)

Chanting arose from the heart of the camp. Rugal and Johan looked at each other, and Johan pressed his lips and nodded. It was time to move. Johan held out his arm, and Treble hopped onto it and climbed to his shoulder. Fascinated by the flutebird's intelligence, Johan had suggested they use Treble as a diversion. Rugal reluctantly agreed after Johan reassured him that no Kargolith would bring harm to a Vellaquar.

Both young men slowly rose to their feet in a half crouch. The moonless night was in their favor as they moved apart, going in opposite directions around the perimeter of tents that marked the edge of the encampment. The border of trees provided additional cover. Soon, Rugal and Johan were positioned on opposite sides, with the sacred court containing the sacred circle at the center.

The light of the campfire ruined Rugal's night vision, and he took a breath, waiting for his eyes to adjust. As his eyes cleared, he could see a covered area extending far enough to hold around twenty people. The covering was made of tanned hides, sewn together with the corners lashed to four wooden poles that were sunk into the ground. In its center was a platform made of what looked to be granite–about two feet high and a diameter of about six feet.

Starting at the edge, rough-hewn benches surrounded the platform, the rows going back to the edge of the cover. Rugal squinted his eyes, trying to make out the details, but it was difficult to see because of the crowd. Symbols of what looked to be a similar script to the message they received when the Ring of Rosin was stolen adorned its sides.

The chanting filled his ears, the strange language increasing his discomfiture. He quickly counted at least fifty people encircling the platform, overflowing from under the cover. He almost gasped out loud when he located Tonar near the front, the two men who had been accompanying him earlier still at his side.

The logical plan of action was for Rugal to get to the sacred circle. If he did, not only could he claim the Rite of Reciprocity and get the Ring of Rosin back, but he could also demand Tonar's release. He could feel his emotions rising and the overwhelming feelings that in the past caused him to run. Recognizing those feelings were without value, he knew he was brave and could face the task ahead.

Rugal decided to implement the Sepharim technique to quiet his mind. Using his five senses, he noted the people swirling around the sacred circle. He closed his eyes. He could hear the rhythmic chanting in his ears. He could smell the smoke from the campfire, its acrid taste in his mouth. He put his hand on the sheath of the sword that the Swordsman had given him, running his finger along its cool surface, and recalled the words the Swordsman had whispered to Rugal right before they had started their journey.

He opened his eyes; his fears melted away as he completely focused on the present. He went over the plan again in his mind, as he waited for Johan to start their diversion.

The chanting stopped, and Rugal drew a breath and tensed slightly, sensing that the diversion was imminent. He was soon proved right, as Treble burst out from the cover of the trees and began circling above the sacred court.

Shouts filled the air:

"Vellaquar!"

"Vellaquar!"

Those in the overflow outside of the cover looked toward the sky–Treble circling close enough to be illuminated by the fire. The Kargoliths that had been seated under the cover sprang up and made their way outside of it to see the wondrous bird. The Kargoliths milled around in confusion as they tried to follow Treble's path in the sky. Rugal saw his opening as all eyes were skyward and leapt from his hiding place.

Moving in a slight crouch, hand on the sheath of his sword, he began to walk rapidly toward the sacred circle, avoiding the milling crowd. It was only a few yards away, and his pulse quickened as the platform that would enable the return of the Ring of Rosin and Tonar's freedom loomed in front of him. One of the elders was still seated, apparently unable to rise on his own. His questioning gaze pierced Rugal, and he called out in a language Rugal could not understand. Not wanting to scare the man but intent on getting to the sacred circle, he paused.

The next moment, he found himself in the dirt, tackled from behind.

Rugal instinctively drew on the training he had received from the Swordsman and rolled away from his attacker and onto his feet, his sword neatly drawn from his sheath and at the ready.

His attacker scrambled up as well and, with head bent, drew his own sword. He raised his face to meet Rugal's gaze, speaking harshly in the same language as the elder.

Rugal almost dropped his sword in shock. "Johan?" he gasped.

The young man before him, looking identical to Johan, lowered his sword slightly and shook his head. He replied cautiously in the same language, and Rugal caught the word, "Rohan."

"You are called Rohan?"

The young man's eyes widened in surprise, and he responded in Rugal's own language. "Yes. I am Johan's birth brother. He is my elder by two minutes."

Rugal stared at Rohan, trying to process what had just happened. The space between him and the sacred circle had filled with more Kargoliths. His opportunity to reach the sacred circle, even if he could get past Rohan, was lost. He looked around and spotted Tonar in the crowd. His two guards had not deserted their post in the excitement and remained on either side of him. Rugal locked eyes with Tonar, and Tonar shook his head firmly. Rugal, anguish in his eyes, turned back to Rohan.

Rohan lowered his voice. "Give my brother my greetings. And do not worry. We will keep your king safe. You must go."

Rugal nodded, glancing once more at the sacred circle that was so close. He sheathed his sword and bolted for the edge of the camp.

Clenching his jaw, once Rugal got to the stand of trees, he turned into a large brown wolf and trotted toward the place where they had left the horses. Treble stayed to circle the encampment a few more times to give Rugal and Johan opportunity to clear the Kargoliths. The new moon was also to their advantage, giving them cover under the darkness.

As Rugal neared the stand of trees where the horses were hobbled, he turned back to human form so as not to startle Flash and Raksh. Both horses were grazing contently, their indistinct shapes a few yards from each other. He waited impatiently for Johan to arrive, striding back and forth and allowing his agitation to grow. Soon, Johan's darkened form came into view.

"What just happened, and who are you?" Rugal demanded, his face flushed and fists clenched. Johan strode quickly to Rugal. "I am sorry, Sire, but we must keep our voices down. I don't think anyone will attempt to follow us under cover of the new moon, but we don't want to invite trouble."

Treble flew through the brisk night air and onto Rugal's shoulder. His comforting presence calmed Rugal's emotions, and he let out a breath. "You're right, of course. But that doesn't answer my question." He gave Johan a piercing look. "Rohan sends his greetings."

Johan rocked back on his heels. "Now I understand. I didn't think he would be here." He returned his gaze to Rugal. "I couldn't see what happened from my vantage point, only that you were unable to enter the sacred circle."

"That is correct. Rohan tackled me from behind. When I regained my feet and attempted to engage him with my sword,

I thought he was you until I heard him speak his name. Imagine my further surprise when he switched from his own language to mine with the same flawless accent that you have and revealed that you are his elder brother." He crossed his arms and waited expectantly.

Johan broke eye contact with Rugal, pacing and rubbing the back of his neck. He looked up and gave Rugal an apologetic smile. "I am sorry, Sire. I did not mean for you to find out this way."

Rugal tapped his foot impatiently. "Find out what?"

Johan looked directly at Rugal. "My name is Johan, but I am not an emissary of King Handerbin of Tolan. My true mission was to capture you and to bring you to the Day of Questioning. I am a prince of the Kargoliths, and my father is chief elder."

Rugal's eyes widened, and he instinctively put his hand on the hilt of his sword and drew it. Their eyes had grown accustomed to the dark, and Johan noted Rugal's change in stance to one of self-defense. Johan held out his hands, well away from his own sword. "Sire, I have no intention of harming you. I never had, truly. I was just trying to do what is best for my people."

Rugal, his body rigid, stared at Johan in disbelief. He fingered the hilt of his sword, trying to decide how to respond. "I trusted you," he threw at Johan, his voice harsh and filled with betrayal.

"And you still can," Johan replied in a desperate voice. "Please, Sire, let me explain."

CHAPTER
FIFTEEN

Pursuing an honorable path is fraught with obstacles but is the only way to true peace.

~ Teaching of the Sepharim

Rugal lowered his sword. "How will I be able to trust anything you have to say? You've led me on a fool's errand and got my closest friend captured. If you are a Kargolith prince, why the need for deception? And why haven't you demanded Tonar's release?" Rugal's face tightened. "You have put those I love in danger. How can you possibly justify that?"

Johan dropped his chin to his chest, lowered his arms, and hugged himself, his lips pressed together. He looked up at Rugal, his eyes wet. He whispered, "I didn't know."

Rugal felt some of the tension drain from his body, and he slid his sword back into its sheath.

"Tell me," He ordered.

"I need to explain about the Kargoliths first," Johan began tentatively.

Rugal, the bitterness of betrayal still welling in him, responded sharply. "Proceed."

"Yes, Sire." Johan licked his lips. "The Kargoliths are a tribe made up of around two thousand people. We are nomadic, encamping at designated places through the cycle of the seasons. In order to more easily support our population, we are broken up into camps of fifty to two hundred, depending on the needs and family makeup of the individual camps. Each camp has sworn its allegiance to the Kargolith leadership, comprised of elders who have been selected by each camp.

"The elders gather once a month at the encampment we just left, at the new moon. It is then that plans are formed for the coming month. Since we are a nomadic culture, our sustenance depends on the weather and the land, so we must plan accordingly each month."

So far, Johan's words corresponded with what Soldar had shared with Rugal during his crash course on the kingdom of Tolan and the Kargoliths after the Ring of Rosin had been stolen. He nodded for Johan to continue.

"We have two factions within the Kargolith tribe. One faction is also called Kargoliths, and we comprise the majority of the tribe, numbering around one thousand four hundred people. The lesser faction, called the Mergoliths, came into our tribe thirty years ago when their numbers were dwindling. Their leaders approached us and asked if they could merge into our larger tribe, to share in our resources. It was a matter of survival for their people, so we agreed."

"So, you are in line to lead the Kargoliths?" Rugal interrupted.

"Yes, that is true. My family line has led the Kargoliths for the past hundred years. My uncle was our leader, but he recently died, leaving no children. My own father is a tribal elder. Because I am nephew and not son, the Mergoliths are attempting to cause dissension for my upcoming appointment to the leadership.

"We are ruled by the elder council, which meets each month. The leader of the Kargoliths can introduce policies and initiate strategies in times of crisis, but in general, the council formulates the plans for how we live and move among each other and the world around us by consensus."

Johan's voice rose. "It is a dream of every Kargolith to have our own territory. We live in limbo between the kingdom of Tolan and the kingdom of Elayas in what you often refer to as the unsettled territory." Johan hesitated. "But it is settled." His voice took on a note of anguish and determination. "By us!"

Rugal could feel his anger beginning to drain slightly, but he could not let loose of it completely, no matter how admirable Johan's motives were. As king, Rugal felt a similar sense of responsibility for his own people, but Johan had deceived him and not only caused Tonar's capture–he did not seek his release when he had the opportunity. Expressionless, he motioned Johan to resume his explanation.

Johan cleared his throat. "The Day of Questioning is our chance to get the information we need to become our own kingdom within the unsettled territory. We will be able to understand what we need to do to convince King Handerbin," Johan paused and glanced entreatingly at Rugal, "And you, to ratify our existence as a sovereign kingdom."

Rubbing the back of his neck, Johan continued. "Our elders deemed the mission to facilitate the Day of Questioning by capturing you too important to have only one plan, and both factions wanted representation. I was sent to represent the Kargoliths and attempt to get you to come through diplomatic means. It is true what I had warned you about. The Kargolith operatives that were sent to kidnap you are the Mergoliths. They also have a deeper motive. The Mergoliths hope to thwart my efforts so that they can gain control of you and forward their own desire to replace my family line with their own and become the leaders of the Kargoliths."

Rugal stepped back, trying to digest all of the outpouring of information. After a few moments, he returned his gaze to Johan. "So why did they kidnap Tonar, and not me?"

"We can thank Rohan for that," Johan replied. For the first time during the conversation, a smile crept onto his lips. "He mistakenly described Tonar to the elders, thinking that he was you. I am not sure why he thought that, but I can assure you, no harm will come to Tonar. Not only do they think we need him for the Day of Questioning, they know they will have no opportunity for peace with Elayas, if he is harmed. We are a proud and determined people, but we also know our limitations." He paused, his expression serious again. "Without your support, we won't be able to exist in peace."

Rugal's voice sharpened. "Why do you think you could gain my support when you planned to kidnap me? And as a Kargolith prince, why didn't you reveal yourself and demand Tonar's release?"

"We couldn't see any other way–the Day of Questioning is rapidly approaching, and that is our chance to finally be in a position of strength. We need you." He paused for breath and continued. "And I know Tonar is safe. They think he is you, and you are essential to our plans. If I had come forward at the camp, I would have been recognized. My honor would not permit me to lie about their mistake and would have put you at risk in exchange for Tonar. You know Tonar would not want that. And you would be forced to comply with their demands. This way, I have given you a choice."

Rugal tilted his head, his eyebrows crinkling as he looked

at Johan curiously. He gestured at Johan. "What about you? Why have you not attempted to catch me off guard and restrain me? Why are you providing me with an opportunity to choose, rather than be coerced?"

Johan bowed his head, shifting his weight as he gathered his thoughts. He finally looked back up. "You've become a friend."

Before Rugal could respond, Treble started flapping his wings in agitation. Flash and Raksh held their heads high, nostrils flaring.

"We better get going," Johan urged Rugal. "It looks like we may have some company if we stay."

Rugal and Johan quickly removed the hobbles from their horses, tightened the girths of their saddles, and mounted. Rugal shoved his anger aside as they focused on getting away. Johan pointed Raksh east, away from the encampment and toward a forested area where they would be able to hide until the Day of Questioning. Any further discussion would have to wait.

Johan's declaration of friendship startled Rugal. He wasn't sure how he felt about that after what had just happened, and he felt a strong desire to talk to Lissa once they found a safe place to camp. The brisk air invigorated all of them, and with their horses having excellent night vision, they soon put any pursuers miles behind.

CHAPTER SIXTEEN

"Johan's perspective makes me examine my own more deeply, and that is a good thing. It helps me to understand why I believe what I do, while also being open to possibilities I may not have considered otherwise."
~ King Rugal

The Day of Questioning is just two days away and I still don't know how I am going to handle it. I don't know if I can trust Johan. Talking to Lissa in his head had been strange at first, but he had quickly grown accustomed to it. He was still dealing with residual anger at Johan's deception. He wriggled against the tree he was sitting against. Johan was in view near the horses but unable to hear the conversation that existed in his mind. Lissa's lilting voice soothed him. *Are the feelings mutual, dearest? Have you come to regard Johan as a friend as well?* Rugal paused, examining his feelings about Johan. He nodded, then felt silly since Lissa couldn't see him, and smiled. *Yes, I believe I have.*

With true friendship comes great responsibility, Lissa observed. *Perhaps you are so angry because his betrayal, no matter how well-intended, is painful. He broke your trust.*

Rugal rubbed his face tiredly. *I think you are right, Lissa. Johan is unlike anyone I have ever known. Not only does he look differently physically–he looks at the world differently.* He sighed. *But it's not bad. It's refreshing. Johan's perspective makes me examine my own more deeply, and that is a good thing. It helps me to understand why I believe what I do, while also being open to possibilities I may not have considered otherwise.* He sighed again and shook his head. *But I can't get over how he just left Tonar there.*

Lissa made a soothing noise. *I understand how frustrated you must be; we all are. We love Tonar, too. But under the circumstances, I think it is a gift.*

Rugal leaned forward, eyebrows raised. "A gift?" he said out loud, startled. Johan glanced in his direction, and he quickly leaned back, returning to the voiceless conversation in his mind. *A gift?*

Yes. Johan and Rohan have both assured you of Tonar's safety, which you have seen with your own eyes. Now, you are unencumbered from being pursued. If you had freed Tonar, the Kargoliths would be swarming desperately to find the King of Elayas. Now, you have breathing room to plan how to best proceed. She paused to emphasize her next words. *And you now have the allegiance of a Kargolith prince to aid you, if you will let him.*

Rugal nodded thoughtfully as he digested the wise words of his beloved. "I am so fortunate to have you," he whispered out loud, with wonder in his voice. He returned to their silent conversation. *I think you are right, Lissa. Johan has risked much–I need to give him a chance.* He could envision Lissa's beautiful hair framing her face, and he smiled. *Thank you, my love. I had better go. We have yet to make our plans, and the Day of Questioning is rapidly approaching.*

RUGAL GOT TO HIS FEET, brushing off the grass clinging to his legs. Johan was just finishing brushing the horses and checking their hooves for any stray stones. A nearby stream allowed them to freshen themselves while providing plenty of cool water to drink. Rugal gathered some dead wood, and they made a fire. They still had dried meat and cheese in their saddle bags, and sitting comfortably on logs, they watched the dancing flames and ate their dinner. The tension from earlier returned, and they sat in awkward silence. Finally, Johan cleared his throat.

"I know you think I betrayed you. I can't blame you for thinking that. I did start out to kidnap you, and I hope you can forgive me." He leaned over and tossed a stick into the fire. "But after I got to know you, I searched for another way. I want our people to be friends, not enemies. I hope you will one day see that I have changed. I am acting out of friendship, and in your best interest." He paused. "Even though it means I may lose my opportunity to claim our territory as our permanent home."

Rugal met Johan's gaze and allowed his expression to soften. "I think I will, Johan. I just need some time. Deception is not easily forgiven, and I am still frustrated we didn't manage to free Tonar."

"I understand," Johan nodded. He leaned forward. "I would like to share with you a fable. It concerns the Ring of Rosin and its special properties. It might also help you understand the relationship my people have with the kingdom of Tolan."

For the first time that day, Rugal managed a smile. Treble gave an encouraging chirp, and they settled in to hear the fable.

The mountains were not for the fainthearted, man or beast. Their rugged beauty attracted some and repelled others. Birds of the mountains were rare and possessed special powers, enabling their survival in the harsh environment. One such bird was called upon to be the keeper of the stone of fire, a huge gem mined from deep in a mountain crevasse. This is the story of two brothers, young men, leaving the safety of home in search of adventure. The peak of the largest mountain loomed far in the distance from their village, and they had determined to climb it one day. They were determined to find the nest of the bird, and steal the stone of fire, for it was said that the stone was imbued with magical power that would be available to whoever possessed it.

When the younger reached the age of manhood, they carefully laid out their plans. They gathered supplies and equipment for their quest and, after saying farewell—with a promise to return after achieving their goal—the two young men mounted their horses and began their journey. Once they entered the mountain range, they carefully picked their way toward the majestic peak that called to them. Arriving at its base, they made camp and planned their ascent for the next morning.

The sun's bright rays woke the two adventurers, and they jumped up, ate a quick breakfast, and prepared for their climb. They hobbled their horses and took packs containing food and water. The terrain was steep and rocky, and they proceeded carefully upward. The sun rose high in the sky as they continued their ascent, their goal a crevasse in the mountain near its peak, where the bird was said to make its home.

The air was cool, and following the advice of the wise men of their tribe who had helped with their preparation, they drank plenty of water. One of the biggest risks at this altitude was dehydration. Looking down, they were astonished to see their horses were tiny dots and the small lake they had camped at was a puddle. They were getting close to the top.

The brothers had climbed in silence, focusing on not slipping on the rocky terrain as they neared their goal. Finally, they saw a crevasse, the home of the great bird of the mountains. Exchanging excited glances, the two brothers made their way to the opening. A precipice at the entrance extended over a darkened cavern, and the brothers paused. The only way into the crevasse was to crawl up the precipice and then drop down into the crevasse.

The two brothers conferred and decided the younger one should go onto the precipice–for he was the lighter and more agile of the two. The younger brother pulled himself up onto the precipice, when a giant bird erupted out of the opening, screaming. The bird knocked the younger brother over as it flew past, the stone of fire in its claws. The older brother had only a second to make a decision–grab the stone of fire from the bird's claws as it flew past or save his younger brother from tumbling to his death.

Johan paused and took a breath. Rugal wriggled with anticipation, his body tense as he waited to hear what the older brother decided. Johan gave a slight smile and continued:

The older brother tried to do both. He grabbed at the stone of fire as the bird flew past–dislodging it from the bird's claws, where it bounced against the mountainside, shattering into pieces. He then swiveled and grasped his younger brother's hand to prevent him from falling into the crevasse and flung him to the side of the opening. The bird shrieked in agonized protest as shards flew in different directions, tumbling toward the bottom. The younger brother rolled partway down the mountain and scraped his cheek against a rocky outcropping, which would leave a jagged scar for life, before coming to a stop.

Even though the older brother had saved him, the younger brother was very angry at his older brother. The two argued and, upon returning to their base camp, went their separate ways. Arriving back at their home, the younger brother gathered his possessions and left, heading north. Eventually, he found another settlement and decided to marry and make his new home there, embracing them as his own people.

When the older brother returned home, he stayed there, married, and raised a family. Eventually, known for his bravery and wisdom, he was elevated to tribal leader. As the years passed and crops failed, he convinced the tribal council to adopt a nomadic lifestyle.

Johan leaned back and smiled.

And they took on the name of Kargoliths–which means, in our ancient language–travelers.

Rugal's eyes widened as he absorbed what Johan had just said. "And what about the younger brother?"

Johan's eyes glittered. "His name was Tolan."

Rugal looked at Johan in wonder. "Do you mean, you are related to the people of Tolan?"

Johan shrugged his shoulders noncommittedly. "According to the legends, yes. But not everyone believes the legends."

"Do you?" Rugal asked pointedly.

Johan paused a moment in reflection, narrowing his eyes and biting his lip. He nodded. "I do."

Rugal let out a long breath. "And what about the stone of fire when it was shattered against the side of the mountain. What happened to those shards? And what makes it so powerful? How did the bird get it in the first place?"

Johan waved his hand, playfully shielding his face. "So many questions!" Seeing Rugal's intent look, his expression turned serious, and he continued.

"It is believed that when the foundations of the earth were laid, the stone of fire was created and imbued with magical powers with the intention of aiding kingdoms in ruling peaceably. As you know from the Ring of Rosin, the stone has the ability to recognize the true ruler of a kingdom. Another magical property is what has brought us together–the stone's ability to be able to impart knowledge to the true ruler during the Day of Questioning. No one knows the extent of its powers, but over the years, some of the shards have been recovered, and they have all been found to have these properties. The Ring of Rosin was commissioned by King Rosin to be made from one of those shards."

Johan rubbed his neck wearily. The fire had died down, and he leaned forward, stirring it with a stick before continuing. "You asked how the bird got it. Legend tells us that once it was formed, a magnificent bluebird was attracted by the stone's reflection as it was flying by. It flew down to investigate, and upon finding the large diamond-shaped glowing red stone, it grasped it in its claws, and became its caretaker. Because of years of close proximity to the stone and its magical properties, the bird took on magical properties of its own, growing to gigantic proportions. The bird passed on this magic to its offspring, including its huge size and the ability to make music like you hear from Vellaquar."

Johan lowered his voice. "Sadly, when the stone of fire was shattered, the bird of the mountains flew away, to live in a self-imposed exile. With the stone of fire gone, its offspring returned to normal proportions." He looked at Treble, dozing in his usual place against Rugal's chest. "We believe that flute-birds derive their abilities from their ancestor, the bird of the mountains, keeper of the stone of fire." Johan shook himself and yawned. "But now, my voice is giving out, and we had better get some rest. We will need it for the Day of Questioning."

The two young men banked the fire, and Rugal weaved a protective thread around them. Gathering his blanket about him, Rugal stared up at the night sky. He could almost reach up and touch the stars.

Good night, Lissa.

Good night, dearest.

You were listening for me!

Of course. Always.

I really like your dynamis. He grinned to himself.

I, do, too.

CHAPTER SEVENTEEN

When two friends find forgiveness, the transgression is as far from them as the East is from the West.

~ Saying of Elayas

"We had better come up with a plan," Rugal commented, munching on bread and cheese for breakfast. They had decided to stay where they were, under cover of the forest, until the Day of Questioning. Rugal still had his blanket wrapped around him in the chill morning air, and Treble was burrowed inside it. The flutebird chirped occasionally as Rugal shared bits of bread with him. The two young men sat on the logs they had found the night before that they had dragged to the fire. "I don't know anything about what to expect, and we need to figure out how we are going to rescue Tonar."

Johan rubbed his chin. "Yes, we need to have a plan." He looked at Rugal thoughtfully. "You know, you can use your *dynamis* for this. Your chance to claim the Rite of Reciprocity is gone, and we have nothing to lose now." He paused, his shoulders tense and his eyes glittering. "I have given up the chance to help my people become a kingdom of our own."

Rugal's heart dropped in his chest. Johan had mentioned it yesterday, but Rugal had ignored it, staying focused on his own feelings. He had not allowed himself to grasp the depth of Johan's sacrifice. He got up and walked over to the young man who had become a friend—despite their cultural differences—and grasped his shoulder.

"I'm sorry it had to happen this way, Johan. But I will help you gain the rights to your kingdom, even if I must fight Tolan to do it." Johan's head jerked up at Rugal's words, his eyes moist. He pressed his lips together, unable to speak. "We have a saying in Elayas," Rugal continued. "When two friends find forgiveness, the transgression is as far from them as the East is from the West." Rugal slapped Johan on the back. "Come, we had better get our plans in place."

Johan's shoulders sagged in relief, and he shot Rugal a grateful smile. The two young men sat side by side, and Johan picked up a stick to draw in the dirt. The morning flew by as they mapped out their ideas, and finally, Rugal stood up and stretched. "I don't know if we'll be able to pull it off, but I think that's got as good a chance as any." He smiled. "Let's take Raksh and Flash for a ride. I think that will help us all settle down." Johan jumped up in agreement, and they headed to the horses, Treble flying above them, chirping happily.

RAKSH AND FLASH jigged about on the trail, feeding off the emotions of their riders. Raksh was trotting behind Flash, shaking his head, eager to get ahead. Rugal turned in his saddle and grinned at Johan, his eyes sparkling. "Shall we race?"

Johan reluctantly kept Raksh reined in and shook his head. "As much as I would like to, I don't want to risk running into a Kargolith camp. My people can be very widespread, and I have not been in this area for a long time." He rubbed his cheek thoughtfully. "As far as they know, you are King Rugal's companion and tried to rescue him. My whereabouts should be unknown. My people will assume I left you since they stole King Rugal away from me when you and Tonar and I were traveling together."

Rugal nodded. "I understand. Sometimes, we must make responsible choices. The burden of leadership," he sighed.

Before Johan could respond, a sharp buzz rent the air, and an arrow flew toward Rugal's chest. Instinctively, Rugal responded to the prompting of his *dynamis* and turned sideways. The arrow narrowly missed him, embedding itself in the tree next to Flash. The big red horse reared and neighed, wheeling off to one side. Johan instinctively pulled the arrow out of the tree trunk as Raksh followed Flash deeper into the woods. "I guess we are going to have that gallop after all," Rugal muttered, as both horses plunged headlong down a faint trail, the sound of hoofbeats not far behind.

"Do you know who that was?" Rugal yelled, crouching low on Flash's neck as the horses galloped through the dense brush, dodging trees as they continued through the forest.

"I don't know," Johan shouted back breathlessly, holding onto Raksh's mane as his brave steed leapt over a log. "I grabbed the arrow. Maybe it will tell us its owner's identity."

The sound of rushing water diverted Rugal's attention, and he peered forward. "A swift-flowing river lies ahead! I don't see any other way–we'll have to go through it."

"I guess now is not the best time to tell you I can't swim very well," Johan replied nervously.

"But Raksh can. Hold on tight!"

The two riders grasped their horses' manes and urged them into the surging rapids. The current was strong, and Raksh and Flash valiantly swam against it, their strong muscular chests cutting through the current as they pumped their legs. They could see the faraway bank, and stayed focused on its stony surface, the forest brush overhanging its sides.

Halfway across, Raksh got caught in the current sideways, and his head went under. He attempted to rear back up out of the water and fell over on his side, dislodging Johan from his seat. Johan struggled, refusing to release the arrow that could identify their attacker, and found himself caught by the current–being swept rapidly downstream.

Flash continued to fight the current ahead of Raksh and managed to scramble onto the far bank. Rugal looked back across the river and saw a figure on a horse staring over the raging water at him. The distance was too great to make out any features, but Rugal shivered, feeling the malevolence of the stranger's gaze, even across the crashing waves. The figure raised his bow as if to shoot again, but instead, put it back down, wheeled his horse, and galloped away from the river. Rugal could feel the malevolence fade as the horse and rider disappeared into the woods.

Raksh managed to right himself and scramble to the bank several yards downstream and began to neigh anxiously. Rugal, unaware of what had happened to Johan, spotted Raksh and looked downstream. He could just make out Johan, grasping a branch hanging low over the river, waves crashing against him as the river continued to rush by him. Pushing aside any further thought about what he had witnessed and felt regarding the evil rider for later–he turned Flash and galloped down the bank toward Johan.

CHAPTER EIGHTEEN

Expect the best, but prepare for the worst.
~ Tenet of the Sepharim

Johan held on tightly to the branch, his face pale as the white water slammed into his body. Beginning to lose his grip, he put the arrow between his teeth so he could hold on with both hands, when a fierce bird of prey grabbed his shoulders. The bird pulled him into the air, and he could feel its fierce claws piercing the leather of his tunic. The huge bird's wings beat strongly upward, and Johan was carried along much like a rabbit in its strong grip. Trembling, Johan grasped the arrow from his mouth and held onto it as the bird made its way to the bank. The bird hovered over the rocks lining the river, opening its claws in a flat area, and Johan tossed the arrow to the shore and dropped in a heap to the ground. He drew himself to his knees, holding his arm over his face to protect himself from the bird's attack. Peering up at the bird hovering next to him, he fell back over onto the ground in shock as the bird transformed into the familiar figure of Rugal, reaching toward him in concern.

"What...How...," Johan slowly got up, arm extended as if to stop Rugal from coming near.

"I can also transform into birds, not just four-legged animals," Rugal held both hands up, palms open in a non-threatening pose. "I know it can be scary–I was very scared the first time it happened."

Johan's shoulders relaxed a tiny bit, and he dropped his arm. "I guess I should be thanking you for saving me." He looked down at his dripping clothes and back at Rugal, his forehead creased in puzzlement. "How could you possibly carry my weight?"

"Normally, I couldn't. Even a bird of prey, which seemed to me the fastest way to rescue you from the river, would not have had enough strength on its own." He patted the sheath that hung at his side. "But I had an advantage. The Swordsman had the Key of Power sewn into the lining of the sheath for the sword he loaned me."

Johan tilted his head to the side and pursed his lips. "I don't understand," he admitted.

Rugal nodded. "It is a lot. Let's get the horses and start a fire. We need to get you out of those wet clothes and get them dried. I'll explain later."

Johan nodded his agreement, then jerked back, hesitating. "Did you see our pursuer?"

Rugal frowned. "I did." He gazed back toward the far bank of the river and then returned his attention to Johan. "I just got a glimpse. When he got to the river's bank, the rider did not try to urge his horse into it. He looked like he was going to shoot an arrow at us but changed his mind and galloped back into the woods. I don't think he is following us any longer," leaving unspoken the presence of evil he felt at their attacker's gaze, and how it had departed with him. He wasn't sure he understood it, and right now, they needed to get the horses and attend to Johan's physical needs. "I don't think he is going to chase us anymore, now that we are on this side of the river."

Johan looked around. "We have to find his arrow. It's our only chance to identify him. I flung it onto the bank when you were rescuing me."

Rugal and Johan started searching in the nearby brush, and Rugal almost bumped into Johan when he came to an abrupt halt. The arrow had landed on a rock. Letting out a huge breath, Johan strode to the rock and picked it up. His eyebrows crinkled in puzzlement. "Strange, it feels warm to the touch," he muttered. "We need to examine it more closely."

"Agreed, but it can wait. I don't want the horses to wander too far, and we..." before he could finish his sentence, Raksh and Flash trotted up to the young men, and pushed their heads into their chests, nickering. Rugal and Johan looked at each other with grins. Their faithful steeds had chosen to stay with them. Finally, a good omen for their journey.

Johan stuck the arrow in his belt. "Well, then, a fire sounds really good right now." He stroked Raksh's neck, then pulled himself into the saddle and gathered up the reins.

Flash shoved Rugal with his nose as if to say, "What are you waiting for?" Laughing, Rugal gave Flash an affectionate slap on the muscular neck, grabbed his mane, and swung onto his back. He looked around and was relieved to see Treble winging toward him. He held up his arm and the flutebird landed gracefully on it, then hopped to his shoulder. "We can't return to camp. We have to stay on this side of the river," Rugal commented. "Whoever shot the arrow surely has tracked us and may be waiting for our return."

"I agree," Johan rubbed the side of his cheek tiredly. "We

can build a new camp a couple of miles from here. It's only for tonight. We will need to be up at dawn if we are going to get to the location of the Day of Questioning in time to implement our plan."

Rugal's head jerked back as he considered Johan's words. He had been so busy in the moment, focused on escaping the threats they had been facing, rescuing Tonar, and recovering the Ring of Rosin, he had not given any thought to the opportunity that would be opening up to him, if all went as planned tomorrow. He needed to consider what questions he would ask the Ring of Rosin.

And if it didn't go as planned, well, he really didn't want to contemplate what might transpire. Rugal rubbed his eyes. It was happening so fast. An unwelcome but familiar feeling pricked his skin, urging him to run. He shook it off and, instead, focused his attention on the issue at hand, reining Flash to follow as Johan urged Raksh into a trot.

CHAPTER

NINETEEN

"Telling the truth makes everything harder and easier - only then can trust to begin."

~ Savash, tribal elder of the Kargoliths

The fire crackled, and Johan gave a sigh of relief. "I finally feel warm again."

Rugal, sitting across the fire from Johan, rubbed his shoulders. "I didn't get as thoroughly soaked as you, but I am very glad to be dry." He got up and rifled through the pack on his saddle and pulled out the soggy mess that was left of their supplies. The bread was inedible, but he managed to salvage enough dried meat and cheese for their meal. He handed Johan his share and, carrying what was left, sat back down to soak in the fire's warmth, the flames dancing and casting shadows on their faces.

Munching their dinner, Johan broke the companionable silence that had enveloped them. "So, what is this Key of Power you mentioned? How did it help you carry me?" He leaned forward, raising his eyebrows.

"Do you remember when I was astride Tag, and the Swordsman whispered something to me as we were about to leave?"

Johan narrowed his eyes in recollection. "Yes, I had assumed he was giving you some last-minute instructions or information for our journey."

"You are correct. He was informing me that he had the Key of Power sewn into the sheath of the sword he was loaning me. He thought there might be a need." Rugal shook his head in awe. "The Tamadar never fails to amaze me with his foresight. He was right. I was able to draw from the Key of Power to have enough strength to carry you."

Johan rubbed his fingers along each of his shoulders, the indentions of the bird of prey's claws evident in the leather. "You were able to do that through your *dynamis*?"

"I don't understand it completely myself," Rugal admitted. "The Key of Power is one of the three symbols for the office of the King of Elayas. The power must come from me, but the Key of Power increases the strength of my *dynamis*, if it is on my person."

Rugal looked awkwardly at Johan. "It was quite a physical drain. If you could give me a moment, I think I better use a Sepharim technique to ease my weariness."

Johan nodded sympathetically. "Should I leave? Is it dangerous?" he asked, his face wrinkled with concern.

Rugal laughed lightly. "No, stay where you are. It's easy, really." Rugal bent his head in concentration and drew several deep breaths. He stayed silent for the span of a minute, then looked up at Johan. "That's it," he smiled. His eyes were bright, and his former exhaustion had vanished.

Johan's mouth dropped open, and he hurriedly closed it. "That looks very handy," he murmured.

"It is," Rugal agreed. "I don't need it often, but I expended a lot of *dynamis* today." He peered more closely at Johan. "You must be exhausted," he commented with concern.

"Nothing a good night's rest won't fix," Johan cheerfully replied. "But come, tell me about the other two symbols."

"Not much to tell, really. You know I left the Sword of Fate behind–it would have given away my identity with the blue stone on the crosspiece. The stone symbolizes the Sepharim and gives me the power to command them when needed. It has a special power to stay in my grip." He pulled at his sleeve. "I wish I could have brought it, but I am grateful the Swordsman had the foresight to have the Key of Power sewn into the sheath of the sword he loaned me." Rugal's voice trembled slightly. "He is a very wise Tamadar. I don't know what I would have done without it."

"You would have figured out something, I am sure. I'm just glad you didn't turn into a bear again–I would have really been scared," Johan grinned.

Rugal laughed, regaining his composure. "You already know about the Ring of Rosin." Rugal's eyebrows crinkled, and he bit his lip. "Whoever has it must be either waiting for the Day of Questioning to bring it out, or they don't know that it identifies the true King of Elayas. The Ring of Rosin vibrates, creating a beautiful musical sound, when placed on the true king's hand. It serves as proof of my right to rule."

"I think they are waiting," Johan observed. "The Mergoliths don't want to risk losing it to a Kargolith."

"So, it was the Mergoliths that stole the ring?" Rugal leaned forward, tilting his head at Johan. "How did they accomplish that?"

Johan sighed. "They were one step ahead of us. They had

planted a youth with your master jeweler–someone whose responsibility was to run errands and serve as a messenger for him. The youth grew up in the environs of Elayas–his mother is from Farath, and his father is a Mergolith. With the recent restructuring of Elayas, since you overthrew Oldag, he was able to blend in fairly easily. When he applied for the job, the master jeweler had no reason to suspect he was a Mergolith. He was on the job several weeks before the theft."

Rugal cocked an eyebrow. "So why was the note they left behind written in an ancient Tolanese script instead of your language?"

"It was part of our strategy. When the time came to claim our territory, if we could create antagonism between Elayas and Tolan because you thought Tolan was behind the theft, you would be more likely to support our claim, especially since our territory would be the land between your borders." His eyes glittered. "At least that was the idea."

Rugal dug in his pocket and held up the medallion Tonar had torn from his captor's neck. He looked at it closely. "It seems to me this script is not that different from the scroll and the script that is part of the granite platform for the sacred circle." He looked pointedly at Johan, eyebrows raised.

Johan spread out his hands. "Kargoliths and Tolan do seem to share a linguistic history. We use a similar script, but our languages differ."

"Well, at least the mystery is solved." Rugal glanced sideways at Johan with compassion in his eyes. "You have had a rough time of it..."

"My plan was to capture you and then compromise with the Mergoliths since they possess the ring." He sighed. "I was going to appeal to the greater good, but it seems everyone has their own definition of what that means." His shoulders slumped as he contemplated the reality of his position.

Rugal placed his hand on Johan's shoulder. "Don't trouble yourself too much. You are trying to do the right thing for everyone involved–no easy task. We have a good plan. Let's see what tomorrow brings."

Johan bit his lip and nodded. "You're right." He looked over at the arrow where he had left it leaning against a tree. "I wish I knew who was chasing us. That is definitely not a Kargolith arrow."

"Do you recognize where it is from?"

Johan shook his head. "No, it's not from around here, nor Tolan. I wonder where its owner is."

"Nowhere near us," Rugal assured Johan.

"How can you know for sure?" Johan looked at Rugal curiously.

"When I was gazing at him across the river, I sensed his presence. It was pure evil. I would know if he were near." Rugal walked over and picked up the arrow, then let out a yelp, dropping it to the forest floor. The arrow burst into flames, and before they could do anything, it burned completely to ashes, leaving the ground blackened where it had fallen.

Rugal and Johan had both jumped back when the arrow caught on fire and cautiously moved forward to examine the remains. The ashes blew into the wind and disappeared, leaving only a slight trace that the arrow even existed.

Rugal and Johan looked at each other with anxious expressions, then Rugal took a deep breath. "Don't worry, I'll weave another thread of protection around us–I'll know if someone approaches."

Johan breathed a sigh of relief. "We'd best try to sleep then. No use worrying about something that has not come to pass. Hopefully the owner of that arrow is long gone. Tomorrow will bring enough troubles of its own."

CHAPTER

TWENTY

"Be content with the ordinary, but be ready for the extraordinary."
~ Aldon of the Sepharim

Mentally and physically exhausted, and knowing Rugal's *dynamis* would keep them safe, both young men fell asleep, their horses hobbled and resting nearby. After about an hour, Rugal woke up and looked around, then whispered to Treble, who had been sleeping in his blanket. The flutebird got up, stretched his wings, and took off, winging away in the moonlight. Rugal glanced at Johan, who continued to sleep soundly, and fell back asleep.

Soon enough, the morning sun's rays broke through the forest canopy, and Rugal and Johan stirred from their slumber. Rugal stood up and stretched, yawning noisily. "Today is the day. I am looking forward to recovering the Ring of Rosin, rescuing Tonar, and heading back to Elayas." He put his hand out apologetically. “Not that I haven’t enjoyed our journey together, Johan. But it will be good to be home.”

Johan chuckled. “I couldn’t agree with you more, Sire. I, too, am looking forward to life returning to normal.” He rubbed his hand across his forehead and sighed. “Although that may no longer be possible. I am guessing the Mergoliths won’t be very happy when they find out they kidnapped the wrong person.”

Rugal looked at the young man that had become a friend sympathetically. “We can’t please everyone. All we can do is our best to protect our people. The plan we came up with does that. Surely, they’ll be able to see that.”

Johan looked down, shoulders slumping. “I hope so,” he mumbled. He hugged himself, then jumped up energetically. “No use worrying twice.” His eyes brightened, shaking off his bad mood. “Let’s get going. We can eat on the way.”

“How far is the meeting place for the Day of Questioning from here?”

“Not that far–maybe two hours, but we best be in the vicinity as soon as possible. We’ll have to return to the other side of the river, but I know of a bridge that provides a much easier crossing. This is one opportunity we won’t want to miss, or we’ll have to wait ten years for another one.”

Rugal nodded. The thought crossed his mind that they might run into their mysterious attacker again, but he shrugged it off. The aura of evil that emanated from the rider was impossible to mistake. He would have known if the rider was still in the area. “Certainly, Johan. If you don’t mind, I want to have a quick conversation with Lissa.” He gave a weak smile. “I don’t want her mad at me for not telling her what I am doing and that I’m okay.”

Johan laughed. “Even a king has to answer to his lady.” He walked a short distance away to give Rugal some privacy.

"Good morning, Lissa," Rugal whispered, his eyes shining in anticipation of hearing Lissa's voice in his head.

There you are, her sweet musical voice filled his mind, and his heart swelled. *I was afraid to reach out in case it was an inopportune time. Are you okay?*

Yes, love, but I can only talk a moment, Rugal replied eagerly in his mind. *We must resume our journey–the Time of Sun Shadow is this afternoon.*

I understand, came Lissa's quick reply, edged with concern.

Nothing to worry about, Rugal continued. *I have sent Treble on a mission...* He glanced at Johan and quickly finished what he needed to say. Talking in his head was becoming more natural, and he ended the conversation with his beloved reluctantly.

They caught their horses, and after a quick check of their hooves for rocks, Rugal and Johan mounted Flash and Raksh, both horses eager to get started. Johan stopped suddenly and looked around. "Where's Treble?"

Rugal shrugged his shoulders. "He's probably foraging for some breakfast more suited to his taste. He does that sometimes. I'm sure we'll see him eventually."

Johan, noting Rugal's lack of concern, moved Raksh forward, and they made their way through the forest.

THE RIDE to the meeting place passed rapidly, and Rugal and Johan found themselves at the edge of a clearing. Johan signaled for silence and dismounted, pulling out Raksh's hobbles, and motioned to Rugal to do the same. The well-trained horses dropped their heads and began to quietly munch grass.

"We need to proceed on foot from here," Johan whispered.

"It is about a hundred yards that way," he pointed at the other side of the clearing. "The center of the clearing will give us a good view of the sun at its zenith, when the Time of Sun Shadow begins. You will only have about five minutes to ask your questions." He looked around. "We will need to be careful–the Mergoliths and Kargoliths must be in the area by now."

"We still have a couple of hours," Rugal whispered. "Do you think they are close?"

"They would be coming from a different direction. I expect them to come separately, since the winner of the internal struggle for power has yet to be determined. The Mergoliths will have Tonar and the Ring of Rosin." He sighed. "The Kargoliths will be coming prepared for a confrontation."

Rugal squeezed Johan's shoulder. "We, too, have different factions, yet they have all united to restore Elayas. Perhaps the Kargoliths and Mergoliths will do the same."

Johan blew out a long breath. "I hope so." He jerked his head toward a stand of trees. "I heard something." They dropped into a crouch, and skirting the clearing, they moved toward the area where Johan heard the noise. Peering through the branches, they could see a camp with four men. Rugal recognized them as the same men who had been at the Kargolith encampment with Tonar, who was still bound and sitting on a log.

"They must have come ahead of the Kargoliths to position themselves when the Time of Sun Shadow begins," Johan whispered. "I see Tonar and his two guards, and the warrior Dungellan is with them. He still has the pouch with the Ring of Rosin around his neck."

Before Rugal could respond, a movement in the brush to their left distracted him. He turned just in time to see a black wolf leaping through the trees, its strong muscular legs in a full gallop as it propelled itself toward the Mergoliths. It leapt onto the man guarding the Ring of Rosin, and tore the pouch from Dungellan's neck. The wolf dropped its head, its eyes gleaming and the pouch holding the Ring of Rosin in its mouth as it hesitated, trying to determine its best route of escape.

Reflex took over. Rugal transformed into a wolf, his brown fur bristling as he rushed toward the black wolf. He took a mighty leap into the air and slammed his body against the wolf, forcing it to the ground, and tried to grab the pouch in his teeth while the other wolf was off-balance. The black wolf popped back up, snarling, keeping its teeth clamped around the pouch, its forelegs poised for flight.

Rugal opened his jaws and bit the ruff around the black wolf's neck, shaking it fiercely in an attempt to dislodge the pouch from his grip. A rock flew through the air and struck Rugal in the side. He yelped in pain but refused to relinquish his grasp of the black wolf's neck. The two wolves began to roll on the ground, and out of the corner of his eye, Rugal could see Dungellan running toward them with his sword drawn and Johan, head down, running to intercept him.

He heard Johan yell, "Stop! Let him go!" and wondered briefly if he was yelling at him or Dungellan.

He was not going to let the black wolf escape with the Ring of Rosin, and bit deeper, causing the black wolf to fling his body in pain. As the two wolves rolled in the dirt, another figure burst out of the trees and dove at Rugal, grasping his legs and trying to pull him off the black wolf.

Not realizing it was Johan, Dungellan shoved him into the dirt, his forward momentum carrying the huge warrior past Johan to where the wolves were fighting. Dungellan raised his sword, looking for an opening to dispatch the black wolf and retrieve the pouch, but the figure that was grasping Rugal's legs let go and flung himself at the fierce warrior. He screamed, "No! You mustn't harm him!"

Dungellan, using the flat of his sword, struck the young man, knocking him senseless, then turned back to the fierce battle as the two wolves fought for possession of the pouch. Johan stumbled forward, putting himself between Dungellan and the wolves. He drew himself up so that Dungellan could see who he was. "Stop!" He commanded. "Step back."

Dungellan paused and, recognizing Johan, lowered his sword. Johan called to the wolves, still locked in battle. "Rugal. Stop. Zerdin is here. It must be his wolf."

The brown wolf, eyes drawn to the figure of Zerdin unconscious on the ground, stopped scuffling, and Rugal stepped back, releasing his grip but ready to spring again. The black wolf shimmered and transformed into a young man, holding the pouch with the Ring of Rosin in his hand.

CHAPTER TWENTY-ONE

Vellaquar, Vellaquar / Salo Besh Candebar
Bird of the Mountains, Bird of the Mountains / Wondrous creature of blue
~ Children's nursery rhyme, Kargolith tribe

Rugal shimmered, returning to his human form. His eyes flashed. He took in the young man's disheveled appearance from their battle and held out his hand.

"Give me the ring!" he commanded.

The young man looked around. Noting he was completely encircled, his gaze fell to Zerdin, who groaned softly and was starting to stir. He met Rugal's eyes. "You are called Yandin. The Ring of Rosin belongs to Rugal, King of Elayas. It must be restored to him."

Rugal paused, considering the young man's words. "You are correct. It belongs to the King of Elayas." His eyes narrowed. "Who are you, and why do you care?"

The young man let out a breath and drew himself up. "I am Prince Hamideh, son of King Handerbin, of the kingdom of Tolan." He held up the pouch. "The Time of Sun Shadow approaches. The Kargoliths mean to use the ring to gain an advantage over Tolan. I have been tasked to stop it."

"Prince Hamideh's manhood journey," Rugal muttered under his breath, nodding to himself. He returned Prince Hamideh's gaze and then looked down at Zerdin, who remained speechless, taking in what had happened and rubbing his head where Dungellan's blade had caught him. "And who is the man you call Zerdin?" Rugal demanded.

Prince Hamideh glanced at Zerdin, and his eyes softened momentarily with affection. "He is my cousin and most trusted friend. He was assigned by my father to accompany me on my manhood journey."

Rugal nodded, glancing over at Tonar. "It is good to have trusted companions," he said solemnly. He motioned again with his hand, allowing his impatience to show in his expression. "Give me the ring!" he repeated.

"No," Prince Hamideh said stubbornly. "Only to King Rugal."

Rugal's face softened slightly. "I am he."

"No," Dungellan spoke up. "We have King Rugal." He pointed at Tonar, still bound and standing between his two captors.

"No," Johan stepped forward. "You have King Rugal's companion. He speaks truth."

"That's impossible," one of the captors spoke up. "Your own brother, Rohan, identified him. We have King Rugal. You can't do anything with the ring–only King Rugal can facilitate the Time of Sun Shadow and gain its wisdom. You must give us the ring."

Dungellan nodded, raising his sword again.

Johan spoke up. "There is only one way to prove who the true King is. The ring has the power to recognize the true King of Elayas–when placed on his finger, it glows and makes a musical sound that confirms his right to rule. Put the ring on your captive, and we will see if you hold the true king of Elayas."

Prince Hamideh looked at Zerdin, who gave a slight nod. The prince reluctantly dropped the ring in Rugal's outstretched hand. Rugal strode to Tonar and smiled at his friend. "It's good to see you, Tonar." Tonar bowed his head briefly. "Thank you, Sire. I am glad you are safe." He held out his hand, and the circle of men held their breath as Rugal slid the ring onto Tonar's finger. He stepped back and waited. Several seconds elapsed, and nothing happened. For Tonar, the Ring of Rosin behaved like an ordinary ring.

Tonar released the breath he had been holding and removed the ring from his finger. Meeting Rugal's eyes, he asked a silent question, and Rugal inclined his head in acquiescence. Tonar grasped Rugal's hand and slid the Ring of Rosin onto his finger.

The ring glowed on Rugal's finger, and a sweet musical sound filled the air, reaching a crescendo for several seconds before settling back into silence. Dungellan sheathed his sword.

"But why the deception?" Prince Hamideh asked Rugal.

"Someone stole the Ring of Rosin. I have been traveling secretly to recover it. Through a series of events, my companion Tonar was mistaken for me and was captured. Just as Zerdin sought to protect you and your identity, Tonar has done the same for me." He turned toward the Mergoliths with a stern look. "You have stolen my ring and kidnapped my companion, a subject of Elayas."

Johan raised his hand and interrupted. "Forgive me, Sire–but..." he pointed.

Several men on horseback were galloping across the clearing, headed their way.

"It seems the Kargoliths have arrived for the Day of Questioning." Johan raised an eyebrow. "Our plans for you to use your *dynamis* so you won't be recognized will no longer work. It looks like we need a new plan." He glanced up at the sun's position. "And fast!"

THE BAND of Kargoliths galloped up to the group of men. Rohan was riding a big black and white paint horse in the lead, and seeing Johan, he reined the horse in, circling to calm him down. "What's going on?" he called out to his brother. "The Time of Sun Shadow is beginning soon. We must be ready!"

Johan reached up and grabbed the paint horse's reins, stroking his neck to soothe him. "All is not as you thought, little brother. You have mistaken the King of Elayas's companion for the king. The Mergoliths captured the wrong person."

"How could that be?" Rohan's dark features drew up in consternation. "We need the king so we can have the advantage–how else can we stand against the Tolans and gain our own territory?"

Johan patted his brother's leg. "Our initial information described the king's companion, Tonar, instead of the king. Tonar was leading the king's horse, and the horse knew him, and he is of the king's age. He was also wearing red. Our agent made an honest mistake."

The other Kargoliths milled around on their horses,

listening to the conversation. Emotions ran high as Johan revealed they had lost their opportunity, and the Mergoliths watched them warily, torn between their loyalty to the tribe that had taken them in and their desire to take its leadership. Prince Hamideh helped Zerdin up, and Rugal and Tonar moved to stand between them and the Kargoliths on one side and the Mergoliths on the other. The tension intensified as the conflicting factions faced each other, only a thread away from the situation exploding. Prince Hamideh stared at Johan, comprehension dawning as he watched the deference he was given by the Kargoliths.

Prince Hamideh left Zerdin and walked slowly up to Johan, his shoulders stiff. "Who are you?" he asked in a quiet voice.

"I am Johan, prince of the Kargoliths," Johan met the prince of Tolan's gaze squarely. Prince Hamideh pointed at his cheek, to a faint jagged line. "You did this!"

Johan's eyebrows crinkled in puzzlement. "I don't understand. I have never met you before. How could I have done that?"

Hamideh's eyes flashed angrily. "I was born with the mark. It is the sign of our people splitting from yours." He stepped back. "Our grandfathers were brothers," he cried, the anguish in his voice felt in every heart present. "Your grandfather thought the stone of fire more important than my grandfather's life."

Hamideh grabbed the sword of a nearby onlooker and leapt at Johan, who ducked and turned toward Dungellan–who tossed him his sword. The two squared off, and Hamideh called out, "You have destroyed our family with your greed. I heard the stories. My grandfather was heartbroken. He was an outcast because of your grandfather. He had to find a new home away from all of the family he had ever known. He was determined to honor his new family and make them a great kingdom–the kingdom of Tolan." He lunged forward, parrying with his sword.

"Only to live as outcasts ourselves," Johan replied, using his sword defensively, meeting each of Hamideh's thrusts with the steel blade. "We never gained our own territory, yet look at you. Tolan is a great kingdom, and we travel from place to place with no home to call our own." Johan met each parry. "So if it's true and we are brothers, why are we fighting?!"

"Because you hurt us!!!" Hamideh yelled. "We were supposed to be family. You betrayed us."

"So, you hold the fable to be true," Johan lowered his sword. "Sometimes family members hurt each other," he said quietly. He held out a hand beseechingly. "We don't have to hold onto the past. We can make a new beginning."

Prince Hamideh stood poised to attack, then slowly dropped his sword arm to his side. He touched the jagged scar on his cheek and opened his mouth to speak, when they were engulfed by a dark shadow. Flame seared the earth as a giant dragon circled above them, roaring and belching fire, its yellow-green and blue scales glinting in the sunlight. The horses reared in terror, and the Kargoliths dismounted, trying to control their mounts.

"Argothal!" Rugal shouted in relief. Treble had found him, and his dragon friend had agreed to help.

The dragon gave a roar in reply, one gleaming yellow eye aimed toward Rugal, it's huge maw filled with rows of sharp teeth opened in acknowledgment.

Rugal sensed the dynamic had changed. The tension between the factions had dissipated, due to the fight they had just witnessed and now replaced by fear of his dragon friend. He called out, "Please land, Argothal. We haven't much time."

The big dragon ducked his head and circled once more, backwinging to land gracefully in the clearing several yards away. Treble, leaving his perch on Argothal's back, streaked toward Rugal, who instinctively held up his arm for the flute-bird to land.

The Kargoliths and Mergoliths gasped. "It's Vellaquar!!" several shouted. Overcome by both the dragon and the miniature bird of the mountains, the Kargoliths fell to their knees, joined by the Mergoliths. Tonar and Zerdin also kneeled, leaving Rugal, Johan, and Prince Hamideh still standing. Johan started to kneel, but Rugal grabbed his arm. "No," he whispered. "You belong with us."

CHAPTER TWENTY-TWO

"So much unnecessary dissension has occurred due to cultural misunderstandings and prejudice. We must learn to communicate with each other."
~ King Rugal, Day of Questioning

Rugal gazed over the group of men kneeling before them, their heads bowed. Squaring his shoulders, he stepped forward. "You have seen the dragon, who is my friend. You have also seen my friend, whom you call Vellaquar–ancestor to the bird of the mountains in your lore. What you must see now, are the leaders of your people. We are not to be kidnapped or cajoled. Civil war is not the way to obtain power. Power is granted to those who are right and true. You have stolen the Ring of Rosin and have tried to capture me for your own gain."

His voice softened. "For many of you, the cause is just. You seek the betterment of your people. But going about it through deception and ill will helps for nothing." His voice grew firm again. "Before you are the future leaders of the Kargoliths, including the Mergoliths, and the kingdom of Tolan. Men who have worked hard and risked all to get to this place today, in their desire to protect their people. Put aside your petty grievances and look to those who would lead you not only from a position of strength, but righteousness. So much unnecessary dissension has occurred due to cultural misunderstandings and prejudice." He held out his hands. "We must learn to communicate with each other."

He paused and turned his face to Johan, his eyes glittering as he continued speaking. "I have come to know Johan during my journey to recover the Ring of Rosin. Seldom have I met a man so dedicated to the welfare of his people, accompanied by a desire to do what is right–a tension he has lived in for your benefit. Johan had many choices to make during our journey. He has always chosen the honorable one." He looked over at the Mergoliths. "Isn't that what you want for your people?" The Kargoliths and Mergoliths remained kneeling but looked up hesitantly. Rugal could see some of them nodding, including Rohan and Dungellan, and continued.

"Here we have the future king of Tolan. He has come forth risking his life in order to preserve the peace. A leader willing to sacrifice himself," and his gaze shifted to Zerdin, "and one who has earned such loyalty in his followers, is someone worthy of the mantle of leadership." Rugal stepped closer to Johan and Prince Hamideh and clasped their sleeves, swinging their arms high up into the air with his own. They turned and faced the crowd, standing straight and tall, the Ring of Rosin on his hand glowing.

"DON'T LOOK AT THE SUN!"

ROHAN WAVED HIS ARMS FRANTICALLY. "The sun shadow has begun!! Don't look upward, or your eyes will burn in their sockets!!"

Dungellan dragged a large log for Rugal, Johan, and Hamideh to sit on, with the remaining men sitting on the ground around it. They waited for the moment the sun shadow would completely envelope the sun, triggering the time period for questions to start. While they were waiting, Rugal whispered to Hamideh, "Looks like we'll both be sore for a few days." He touched his side where the rock had struck and rubbed his neck gingerly. "How did you transform into a wolf? I was told that *dynamis* is not common in Tolan." Hamideh shrugged, and a mischievous grin crossed his face. "Oldag was not the only Tolanese that possesses *dynamis*. It skipped a generation but runs in my father's line as well."

Rugal sat back in surprise, then leaned forward again. "So how did you learn its mastery? Oldag came to the Sepharim school." He peered closely at Hamideh. "We seem to be close in age. I am quite certain I did not see you there."

Hamideh grinned again. "I think you know my teacher. His given name is Zander."

Rugal's eyes widened. "The Swordsman?" he sputtered.

Hamideh nodded but before he could elaborate, they were interrupted by a shout.

"It's almost time!"

Rugal looked around as the entire sky began to darken.

Everyone stopped talking, and an eerie silence settled over the clearing. The voices of nocturnal animals started drifting through the air. Johan pulled a dark square out of his pocket, and held it up in front of his eyes, then turned his gaze upward, directly at the sun.

"What are you doing?" Rugal stood up. "You will damage your eyes!" Johan put a calming hand up as he continued to look skyward, then dropped his gaze.

"No, Sire. This is a special instrument that has been passed down in our family for generations. It has a magical property that guards the eyes when looking at the sun. When the sun is engulfed by the sun shadow, it is safe to look upon it without any protection, but as soon as even the smallest sliver of the sun becomes observable, you can only look at it safely through this." He handed the dark square to Rugal, who held it skyward and peered toward the sun. He could see the smallest of slivers still evident.

"So, when the sun is completely engulfed in shadow, I begin asking my questions?"

Johan nodded. "Yes, you will have a window of perhaps five minutes to ask and get answers. The Ring of Rosin will stop responding once the sun begins to reveal itself again."

Rugal held the square up again. "I am watching the last of the sun being overcome by the shadow!"

"It is time, Sire." Johan held out his hand for the square. "You must ask now."

Rugal nodded, dropping to his knees and holding the hand that wore the Ring of Rosin out before him, his eyes closed in concentration. The ring began to glow.

"Ring of Rosin, how do I proceed?" Rugal asked in a shaky voice. He gripped his thigh with his other hand, steadying the trembling that threatened to engulf him.

The ring glowed in cadence with the speech emitting from it.

"You may ask any question. I will respond."

Rugal drew a calming breath. "Where does your knowledge come from?"

The ring flared, then settled into the cadence of its speech. *"Wisdom from above."*

Rugal paused, trying to assimilate what was happening, when he felt Johan nudge him and whisper, "Sire, you haven't much time."

Rugal leaned forward, holding the ring so that all could see. He looked at Johan and Hamideh, then returned his gaze to the ring.

"Are the fables true? Are the Kargoliths and Tolans brothers?"

"Yes."

"How can they release past grievances?"

"By looking forward together."

Hamideh and Johan exchanged glances.

"What about the Mergoliths? How can the Kargoliths and Mergoliths resolve their inner strife?"

Johan, Rohan, Dungellan, and the other Kargoliths held their breaths for the answer.

"The Mergoliths are Kargoliths now. They need not forget where they came from, but peace will only come when the Mergoliths fully embrace their new identity and the Kargoliths fully accept them."

"Who is the true leader of the Kargoliths?"

"Johan is the true leader of the Kargoliths."

The Kargoliths let out their breaths, and Rohan moved next to Johan, squeezing his shoulder. Johan took a shaky breath, and returned his attention to the questioning.

"What of the evil rider who shot the arrow at me? Who is he, and will he return?"

"He is evil beyond comprehension and possesses magic through his arrows. He and his people live across the sea. He will return and bring companions with the intent to destroy all of you."

"What is the magic he possesses?"

"His arrows have different properties that he can use for his own means. You saw the fire arrow. When it sensed your dynamis and its evil owner was not present, it disintegrated. That is not the case if he is present. His magic would have caused its flames to spread, engulfing whatever is in its path."

"What is this evil presence called?"

"He is a Neliph, of the Neliphim Clan."

Rugal's hand began to visibly shake. "When are they coming?"

"At the end of winter."

"How can we stop them?"

"Your futures are dependent on your kingdoms working together. You, Johan, and Hamideh are marked, and each of you will have to give up something you hold dear for the greater good. Even so, there are no assurances. The future is cloudy."

Rugal's palms grew sweaty, and he steadied himself, taking a breath before continuing.

"What will we have to give up?"

The glow had faded. The ring was silent.

CHAPTER TWENTY-THREE

Darkness may descend, but light shall overcome it.
~ Kargolith Proverb

Johan pulled out the dark square and raised it skyward. "I can see the sun! The time for questioning has ended."

Rugal fell over onto the ground and closed his eyes as he reviewed in his mind what the ring had revealed. Everyone remained quiet, contemplating the words of the ring, as the sky gradually lightened, and the nocturnal animal voices faded completely away. Finally, Rugal got to his feet. Standing in front of the log, he cleared his throat, capturing the attention of the gathering.

"We have accomplished what we have set out to do. Now it is up to us to use the knowledge that has been gifted to us this day." His eyes moved to each man present, meeting each gaze with his chin proudly raised and a confident expression of affection mixed with determination.

"Each of you has a role to play. You must not only carry the message of what you learned today, you must support what we learned and lead others in doing so." He paused, his expression momentarily grim. "If you do not, the consequences will impact all of us. We must learn to accept one another despite our differences." His voice grew more forceful. "We can celebrate our differences, because when we come together, our differences will make us stronger against any foe." His eyes flashed, and his hand dropped to touch the sheath of his sword. "You heard the ring. We face a common enemy. We must somehow find unity and friendship." He gestured for Johan and Hamideh to stand with him. "What say you, Johan?"

Johan gripped Rugal's arm, squarely meeting his gaze. "The Kargoliths join the kingdom of Elayas in this fight."

Rugal turned to Hamideh. "What say you, Prince Hamideh?"

Hamideh met Rugal's eyes and placed his hand over Johan's. "The kingdom of Tolan joins the Kargoliths," He smiled briefly at Johan, who nodded, "and the kingdom of Elayas in this fight."

"What of the Mergoliths? And territory for the Kargoliths to claim their own?" Dungellan called out.

Johan swiveled toward Dungellan. "Important questions to be sure, Dungellan. I will need your help presenting to the elders what happened here today." He held out his hand. "You are just as much a Kargolith as I am. If you didn't believe it before, the Ring of Rosin has put all doubts to rest. Let us stop making a distinction between how we all became Kargoliths and strive for unity so that we can move forward. Agreed?"

The big man's eyes grew moist, and he nodded. "Yes, Johan." He hesitated, then continued. "The ring has spoken. We will support your confirmation as leader before the council." Before Dungellan could get in another word, Rohan leapt forward, wrapping his arms around the warrior's chest and shoulders, almost knocking him down. "Brother!" he shouted gleefully. The remaining Kargoliths and Mergoliths mingled with one another, slapping backs and shaking hands, as Johan watched with a grateful expression.

"Congratulations, Johan," Rugal whispered. "They are fortunate to have you." He paused and grinned. "And I am fortunate to be your friend."

Johan smiled at Rugal, but then his eyebrows drew together in consternation. He turned to Hamideh. "And what of us? How do we move forward? Prior to today, the revelation of our kinship was considered merely conjecture by my people." He pointed toward the scar on Hamideh's face. "But the ring has confirmed your claim."

Hamideh contemplated Johan's words for a moment, his eye looking into the distance. He refocused on Johan. "It seems we have much to talk about. I never dreamed my manhood journey would bring me to this place. I will need to bring this news to my father. For now, I pledge to follow the wisdom of the ring. We will find a way to put aside past grievances and look forward together."

Johan nodded. "And a territory to call our own?"

Rugal met Prince Hamideh's eyes. "Do you promise to seek a compromise with the Kargoliths, so they can have full claim to their own territory, allowing myself to mediate a treaty that all parties can agree to?"

Prince Hamideh turned to Johan. "I can't speak for my father, Johan, but he is a reasonable man. The goal of my manhood journey was to secure our kingdom's borders from you by stealing the Ring of Rosin, so that you would not have an advantage over us from the questions you asked. I think I have gained much more than expected, and my father will be pleased. I have come to know you, and we have found out from the ring that we have a shared heritage." He grinned. "We may even be cousins. I will keep my promise and work for a mutually beneficial treaty to define the borders of Tolan and the unsettled territory, so that your claim is defined for all to accept as the kingdom of Kargolith."

Johan looked over at his people, kneeling and watching. "Finally, a home of our own," he said hoarsely, eyes shining. He swallowed hard, then grinned. He turned back to Prince Hamideh and grasped his arm. "We would be honored." He leaned forward and embraced Hamideh, the young prince returning his hug. They pounded each other on the back–long-lost relatives celebrating their reunion. The men rose to their feet and gave a mighty cheer, their voices echoing through the clearing.

The excitement of the revelations that occurred during the Time of Sun Shadow and their responses to those revelations left everyone drained. Camp was made in the clearing for the evening, and in the morning, the various factions would depart for home, bringing news of what had happened with them. Flash and Raksh were hobbled and grazing with the other horses, and Argothal made himself comfortable at the far edge of the clearing, Treble perched to rest on one of his scales. Rugal leaned against a tree trunk, physically, mentally, and emotionally exhausted. He smiled as he felt the now-familiar tickle of Lissa, communicating in his head.

It is finished, dearest. All is well. Rugal smiled, picturing Lissa's flowing hair and the sweet expression on her face that she saved only for him.

What happened? Did the Ring of Rosin respond to your questions?

Beyond what I could have imagined. I have much to share, but I will be home soon. Argothal will be transporting me back to Cargoa in the morning. His eyes lit up. *I will be home in time for lunch.*

That will be wonderful, Lissa quickly responded. *What of Tonar? How will he be getting home?*

One of the things Rugal loved best about Lissa was her concern for others. *No worries there, my love. Tonar will be riding my new steed, Flash, back to Cargoa. You will like him–he is well-trained and has become a faithful friend. Johan must return to the Kargolith encampment to share the news of the Ring of Rosin's revelations with his people. But his brother Rohan has agreed to accompany Tonar back to Cargoa. Rohan will serve as the Kargolith diplomatic emissary to Elayas.* He sighed. *So much to go over, my love. But it will all become clear when I return.*

He didn't want to reveal what he had learned about the rider with the arrow, the Order of the Neliphim, and the looming threat to all of them until he was there in person, with his council gathered about him. He would need every bit of wisdom he could garner from his advisors as to how to move forward–no need to alarm Lissa unnecessarily with the news beforehand. It was still summer. They had time to prepare.

And what of Prince Hamideh? Is he coming here or returning home?

Prince Hamideh also has much news to share with his father, and a celebration will be prepared for the successful completion of his manhood journey. He will be returning to Tolan, but I have a feeling we will hear from him very soon.

It sounds like you have things well in hand. I can't wait to see you.

Rugal allowed himself to enjoy the tingly feeling he always got when talking to his future queen. *I can't wait either. Please tell everyone of my homecoming. The Ring of Rosin is safe with me, and I have much news to share. Until tomorrow, my love.*

Rugal sat up and looked around, observing the men scattered about the camp, wrapped in blankets under the starry sky. He looked down at the Ring of Rosin on his finger, lightly glowing in response to his gaze, then fading back into its natural reddish color. He could feel the comforting presence of the Key of Power in the sheath of his sword. His gaze shifted to Johan and Hamideh, both asleep in close proximity to one another, as cousins would do. He picked up his own tattered blanket and wrapped himself in it. He closed his eyes and, for the first time since their journey began, fell into a truly peaceful sleep.

CHAPTER TWENTY-FOUR

"The future is not known; tomorrow is not promised. Live your best in the moment you are in."
~ Raza, philosopher of Tolan

Mura and Jackal sat in the cushioned chairs in the library near the fireplace. The Swordsman pulled up a hardbacked chair in their vicinity and eased his large frame into it. Lissa stood near the table and kept glancing at the doors. The logs crackled cheerily. Even though it was still summer, the inner castle could get chilly, and the dancing flames provided a welcoming ambiance.

Rugal?

Even in his head, he could hear the anxiety in her voice. *Don't worry, Lissa. I am just saying goodbye to Argothal, I will be there momentarily.*

Yes, of course, Lissa sighed with relief. "Rugal will be here soon," she informed the others.

Jackal and Mura exchanged understanding glances. They had experienced many separations throughout their relationship, sacrificing time together as they sought to free Elayas from Oldag's tyrannical reign. Mura smiled affectionately at her future daughter-in-law. "I am sure he is just as anxious to see you, my dear. But dragons do hold a certain charm."

Lissa's cheeks reddened, and she looked down and smiled. "I have been found out."

"We wouldn't want it any other way," Jackal soothed. Before anything else could be said, the doors to the library burst open, and Rugal came striding through.

Lissa ran to meet him, and he hugged her fiercely, before pulling back. "I have missed you so much!" he exclaimed. He kept his arm about her shoulders and turned to the others, who were all smiling at the reunion. His face was glowing, as it always did when he got to ride a dragon.

"Glad to have you back home, son," Jackal called out, standing up. Mura, her cheeks suddenly damp, also stood and reached out a hand. Rugal, carrying Lissa along, moved forward to squeeze it.

"Mother," he smiled. "Don't worry, I am in one piece." He grinned. "And I have found my own way." He paused. "Although I almost didn't make it from the courtyard," he laughed. "Yandin practically tackled me, he was so excited I've returned."

Mura smiled, her eyes shining. "My frog has come home," she laughed, remembering that moment just a few short months ago when her son had run away in frustration, and she had found him at the river of Selba. "Yandin is excelling in his apprenticeship. He is loyal and hardworking and will make a fine royal blacksmith."

Rugal winked, then looked mournful. "Can we get some food brought in? I have much to share, but Argothal didn't stop for lunch." Treble chose that moment to make his entrance, flying into the room and landing on Rugal's shoulder, squawking his agreement.

"Of course," the Swordsman laughed. He had also gotten up from his chair when Rugal entered. Slapping Rugal on the back affectionately, he headed for the door. "No one else has eaten either. We wanted to wait for your return. I'll request lunch to be brought here for all of us, including Treble."

WITH THE LAST of the food still strewn across the table and everyone feeling satisfied at the ample lunch Melad's staff had provided, they all leaned in for Rugal to share what had happened during his journey.

Rugal held up his hand, smiling broadly. The Ring of Rosin glowed momentarily, then resumed its normal state. "It has been quite an adventure," he said. "I am not even sure where to begin."

Mura raised her eyebrows at her son, her eyes glowing with affection. "How about at the beginning?" she asked drolly.

Rugal laughed. "Of course, Mother. You will want to settle in. There's a lot to tell." He took Lissa's hand and squeezed it. "It's good to be home. So, I will start with Tonar's kidnapping. As you know, the Swordsman had seen Johan, Tonar, and I off. We began our journey with Johan as our guide leading us..."

Two hours later, Rugal got up and stretched. "And now, I am here with my family, my favorite place to be."

Jackal stood up from his chair and moved to embrace his son. "Mura and I are so proud of you. Felan would be, too," he murmured and stepped back, his eyes moist. He sat back down and clasped Mura's hand.

"Thank you, Father," Rugal briefly bowed his head and smiled.

Rugal turned to the Swordsman, and a mischievous grin crossed his face. "What a fine opportunity for you to elaborate on your relationship with Hamideh."

The Swordsman jerked his head up, startled, then settled back into his chair with a sigh. "Yes, Sire," he agreed. "It's really quite simple." He looked off into the distance, eyes narrowed in thought, then began to speak. "As you know, I have no family, but I did at one time. Our family lived in a village too small to even be named, just north of Farath and on the border of the unsettled territory. During Oldag's reign, marauders were not uncommon."

He turned to Jackal and Mura. "Do you recall the drought the year before Rugal's birth?" They nodded, and he continued. "That was the year my village was assaulted. A group of men had come to our village, seeking food and shelter. We welcomed them into our homes, and even though we were suffering from the drought, we shared what we had.

"We needed food, so I left on a hunting trip, leaving my parents and my younger sister at home."

The pain in his eyes was so evident, Mura got up and rested her hand on his arm. "You don't have to do this," she whispered.

The Swordsman shook his head. "But I do. And it helps to share my story with those who love me. I feel safe here." Mura nodded, gave his arm a gentle squeeze, and sat back down.

The Swordsman looked at each of his audience with an unreadable expression, his emotions roiling below the surface, and continued. "When I returned from the hunting trip, the village was gone."

Rugal's eyebrows crinkled. "What do you mean, gone?"

"I mean, everything had been burned to the ground. Our homes, shops, and fields. Anything of value was gone."

"What about the people?" Lissa whispered.

The Swordsman bowed his head. "I don't know. I never saw them again."

Mura, Jackal, Rugal, and Lissa all stood up and gathered around the Swordsman, who sat looking down in his chair. They reached out their hands, touching his shoulders, trying to convey their sympathy.

Mura finally spoke. "We are so sorry you experienced the loss of your family. We are very grateful you are part of ours." The Swordsman looked at the faces of those surrounding him and managed to put on a tearful smile. The tension left his body. "Thank you," he breathed.

Returning to their seats, Mura asked gently, "Do you want to continue?"

The Swordsman cleared his throat and nodded. "Yes. I'm okay." He smiled. "It's good to talk about it." He resettled himself in his chair and continued. "My father possessed *dynamis.* Because of the drought, I was unable to attend the Sepharim school–my family needed me. But my father had been to the school, and he taught me everything he knew." He looked down, his voice shaky. "I was so affected by the betrayal of men we had not only trusted but had shared our homes and food with, that I could not trust anyone. For a few years, I lived in the woods north of Farath, near where my village once stood.

"One day, while out hunting, I ran across a young boy. He was alone in the forest, and he looked scared. My first thought was to leave him, for he was no business of mine. I had not been around people in so long and had no desire to. But he was obviously in distress. Reluctantly, I approached him and found out he was lost. He had snuck his horse out for a ride, and the horse spooked at a bear while they were running down the trail. He wasn't ready and fell off. His horse kept running, and he was alone. He was also very ill-prepared to be in the forest."

The Swordsman took a breath and continued. "I couldn't leave him there by himself. He wasn't sure of the way home on foot but knew it was north, so we set out on the trail northward. At one point, I had to use my *dynamis* to shield us from the bear; the trail went by her den and two cubs. After a couple of hours, a huge group of horsemen came thundering down the trail. The young boy's horse had headed home, and when he appeared riderless, the royal guard jumped on their horses and headed our way. Before I knew it, I was facing men on horseback with swords unsheathed and bows drawn. The young boy leapt in front of me with his arms outstretched. I was amazed at the transformation from a scared young child to a confident boy with command in his voice. 'Do not harm him. He saved me from the forest.'"

The Swordsman rubbed the back of his neck. "Long story short, the young boy was Prince Hamideh. He invited me to work at the castle as a huntsman. Because of him, I slowly learned to trust again. When his *dynamis* revealed itself, King Handerbin asked me to teach Hamideh the ways of the Sepharim that I had learned from my father. In doing so, I realized I wanted to attend the Sepharim school myself to become more complete in my learning, so after I taught Prince Hamideh all I knew, I left Tolan and returned to Elayas. I entered the Sepharim school and immersed myself in its teachings. My mentor was Philaten, the Tamadar before me. I eventually met Jackal," he paused to smile at his friend, "and you know the rest."

"Thank you for sharing your story," Rugal said with affection in his voice. "I am grateful for your service to Elayas and your friendship. I couldn't have become king nor lead Elayas well without you."

The Swordsman blushed, then cleared his throat, intentionally shifting the conversation. "But please, may I see if I understand the main points from your journey correctly? It is important for the Sepharim to update their information accurately."

Rugal inclined his head. "Of course."

The big man held up his hand, raising a finger for each point he expressed.

"One, the Kargoliths are actually made up of two factions. The dominant faction is called the Kargoliths. The Mergoliths merged with the Kargoliths when the Mergoliths were in distress, but both Kargoliths and Mergoliths still maintain their separate identities. In the past, there has been some civil unrest because the Mergoliths did not fully integrate into Kargolith society."

"Yes, that is correct," Rugal replied.

The Swordsman rubbed his chin thoughtfully. "That matches up with the reports of our Sepharim agents in the field. So, two, the Mergoliths wanted to steal the Ring of Rosin and kidnap the king of Elayas to gain an advantage over the Kargoliths at the Day of Questioning, perhaps changing the balance of power in their favor. In doing so, they would secure the means for getting the information they would need to force Tolan to recognize the Kargolith claim to the unsettled territory–is that correct as well?"

Rugal nodded. "So far, so good."

The Swordsman continued, "And three, the Mergoliths accidentally captured Tonar instead of you, although they did manage to steal the Ring of Rosin. They arrived at the Day of Questioning, not knowing they had the wrong person. You arrived with Johan, and the Ring of Rosin identified you as the true king of Elayas. Afterward, the time for questioning the Ring of Rosin, called the Time of Sun Shadow, commenced."

The Swordsman paused, and Rugal nodded his affirmation again, gesturing for him to keep going.

The Swordsman took a breath and continued, "Long story short, what you found out during the Time of Sun Shadow is that the Mergoliths and Kargoliths, while not forgetting where they came from, should embrace each other as one people. That is the only way they will be able to move forward. Johan is a prince of the Kargoliths and the true leader of his people.

"The Tolans and the Kargoliths share a common ancestry in the two brothers that sought the stone of fire–the fable is true.

"Prince Hamideh of Tolan has successfully completed his manhood journey and is committed to helping the Kargoliths become recognized as their own kingdom with their own territory."

"I did leave one thing out," Rugal admitted. "I was so happy to be home, I didn't want to bring it up quite yet. Do you recall that Johan and I were attacked by what we assumed was a marauder? The one that shot an arrow at me." The Ring of Rosin's words were burned into his brain. "I asked the Ring of Rosin to reveal his true identity, and it did." Rugal closed his eyes and recited:

> *He is evil beyond comprehension and possesses magic through his arrows. He and his people live across the sea. He will return and bring companions with the intent to destroy all of you. Your futures are dependent on your kingdoms working together. You, Johan, and Hamideh are marked, and each of you will have to give up something you hold dear for the greater good. Even so, there are no assurances. The future is cloudy.*

Their earlier joyous mood at being reunited disintegrated as Rugal's words hung in the air. Rugal stood up and gazed at the people he loved, who looked back with varying degrees of dismay. "The Ring revealed that he is a Neliph, of the Neliphim Clan. They will not be coming until the end of winter. Prince Johan, Prince Hamideh, and I have pledged to work together against this threat. The future may be cloudy, but we have overcome so much already. I believe we will be able to triumph over evil again." He searched each face. "Believe with me!"

Rugal's words did much to relieve the tension that had filled the room, but with so much at stake, it didn't dissipate completely. It may only be midsummer, but the end of winter would arrive before they knew it.

CHAPTER TWENTY-FIVE

"We must learn to accept one another despite our differences. We can celebrate our differences, because when we come together, our differences will make us stronger."
~ King Rugal

"Just put your foot there," Rugal pointed at Argothal's foreleg. Lissa hesitated, and Rugal grasped her arm to provide balance. "Don't worry, you won't hurt him," Rugal encouraged the future queen of Elayas.

Argothal craned his head around and looked at Lissa, his yellow eyes gleaming, and his huge jaw relaxed. *I am happy to transport you.*

Lissa gasped, almost pulling Rugal over as she backed up and put her hand to her mouth. "I can hear you!"

Argothal regarded her calmly, tucking in his wings. *Of course you can. Your dynamis is powerful. You are Ethiod's daughter, after all.*

But why could I not hear you when I was visiting my father?

Argothal opened his mouth in the equivalent of a dragonly smile. *Your gift had not emerged yet–remember?*

Oh, yes, Argothal, Lissa nodded. *You are right.* She paused, eyes narrowed. *I have no idea the extent of my gift. So far, it is only you and Rugal.*

"Are you okay?" Rugal asked. He was trying to be patient, but he was eager to get going.

"Oh, yes! I can hear Argothal!"

Rugal shoved down a jealous twinge and swallowed. "That's great!" he managed to reply.

Lissa leapt onto Argothal's foreleg, and grabbing convenient scales, she climbed onto his back and sat where Rugal indicated. Rugal shook his head wryly. His betrothed never ceased to surprise him. He leapt into place in front of Lissa, and Treble took his place on the dragon's neck.

"If you please, Argothal, we are ready," Rugal urged. The giant dragon untucked his wings and positioned himself into a crouch, leaping skyward. Rugal turned his head–a big grin on his face. "You are doing great!" Rugal yelled.

Lissa's face glowed, and she returned his grin, patting the scale in front of her. "Argothal says we'll be at the king's castle in Tolan by midday."

Rugal nodded and turned, facing forward again, feeling the wind whip through his hair and the joy he always felt riding a dragon. He was so glad Prince Hamideh invited him and Lissa to the celebration marking the successful completion of his manhood journey. Tonar and Rohan had arrived in Cargoa the day before and would be at the castle upon his return. After the events of the past two weeks, it was good to take a trip with his beloved to help a friend celebrate his accomplishment.

Despite their cultural differences, Prince Hamideh had become a friend in their time together. He hoped that Johan was attending as well. The Ring of Rosin showed their destinies were intertwined, and while they would be there to celebrate, they should also make plans. The mantle of leadership always existed, despite their own personal desires.

"THAT WAS QUITE A CEREMONY," Rugal slapped his friend on the back. "Congratulations on your new status and the announcement of your upcoming coronation!"

Hamideh's face split into a wide grin, and he bounced on his toes. "I am so glad you could be here to share in it. Father has worked hard for many years, and now that I have completed my manhood journey, he is ready to pass on the reins. I am fortunate he will still remain here as an advisor, and I can benefit from his wisdom." He looked around. "Where's Lissa?"

"Oh, she is quite taken with your little sister. She and Gillian are enjoying exploring the meadow around the castle." He looked over at Johan and back at Hamideh. "She also knows we need some time together."

"Yes," Johan agreed. "I also have good news to share. The tribal elders have voted and have formally appointed me as leader of the Kargoliths. The Mergoliths on the council cast their votes, and the results were unanimous." His face lit up, joy shining in his eyes. "We are moving forward as one people." He turned to Hamideh. "And everyone is excited at the revelation that the fable of the Bird of the Mountains and the Stone of Fire is true. That the Kargoliths are related to the people of the kingdom of Tolan!"

Hamideh clasped his hand to his heart. "Yes, Tolan is excited as well. I think that knowledge will help pave the way to declare a territory for the Kargoliths to claim as their own."

Rugal beamed and pumped his fist. "Good news all around!" His tone turned serious. "But we need to make plans to defend our kingdoms from the evil one plotting to arrive at the end of winter and destroy us. I think a great start would be the Sepharim ceremony that would bind us together as brothers. What do you think?"

Johan cleared his throat uncomfortably. "I am willing, of course, but I possess no *dynamis*. Would the ceremony be legitimate? Or even doable?"

Rugal gazed at Johan with a kind expression. "Don't worry, Johan. It is very doable. It does not require all of the participants to possess *dynamis*, just willing hearts."

Johan lifted his chin and, smiling broadly, met Rugal's gaze. "Then, I'm in!"

They both turned with questioning looks to Hamideh, grinning from ear to ear. "Of course," he shouted. "I'm in!" He paused, thinking. "So when shall we do the ceremony?"

"At nightfall, if that works for both of you. We could slip away after dinner before the evening festivities begin."

"Will we need anything?" Hamideh asked.

"The weather looks clear," Rugal observed. "We could do the ceremony in the meadow. Nothing special is needed."

"That sounds perfect," Hamideh said, and Johan nodded in agreement. "Uhhhh...one more thing," the young Tolan prince smiled shyly.

Rugal turned to Hamideh and gestured encouragingly.

The words came rushing out, "Can I ride Argothal?" he asked eagerly.

Rugal glanced at Johan standing nearby. The Kargolith prince also had a hopeful expression on his face. He laughed.

"We have an ancient proverb: *Never pass up the opportunity to ride a dragon.* Let's go ask Argothal and see!"

CHAPTER
TWENTY-SIX

Three people are like a rope with three strands wrapped together. It is very hard to break.
~ Kargolith Saying

The stars shone brightly through the pinholes of the night sky's deep blue canvas. Rugal was kneeling and feeding a fire when Johan and Hamideh gathered around it. The area had obviously been designated as a place for evening refreshment and was clear of debris, with logs for sitting scattered about and a stack of dried branches to fuel a fire off to one side. Rugal looked up and smiled at their approach.

"Perfect timing, I am almost done."

He fed a few more branches into the fire, then stood up and dusted himself off. "Let's form a triangle around the fire," he instructed.

They each pulled up a log and sat in the moonlight, staring

into the blaze. Rugal let some time pass as they each contemplated the flames. After a few minutes, he cleared his throat, and Johan and Hamideh drew out of their reveries and focused on him.

"I know we all have much to think about," Rugal began. He rubbed his cheek. "It has truly been an extraordinary journey, beginning with Johan appearing at the castle in Cargoa," he winked at Johan and continued. "Throughout my life, I have been surrounded by my countrymen. The people of Elayas and her unique culture. Once I found out I was the rightful heir to the throne, my education began, and I was totally immersed in learning everything that had to do with Elayas." He took a breath. "I couldn't think of any other kingdom or people because we were fighting to restore our own kingdom." He paused to stretch, and he gazed across the fire at Johan, then Hamideh. "For the first time, when the Ring of Rosin was stolen, I encountered cultures different from my own." He looked down for a moment. "I must admit I was scared of you." He looked back up. "I was scared because you are different from me."

Johan murmured, "I felt the same about you, Sire," and Hamideh bobbed his head in agreement.

Rugal nodded understandingly. "But here is what happened as we journeyed together," he diverted his gaze to Johan, "and when I understood the loyalty you inspired in Zerdin and your willingness to sacrifice yourself," Rugal looked at Hamideh. "I found that we have more in common than we are different." He took another breath. "And that when we open our hearts and minds to those who are different from us, we are richer for it."

Rugal's eyes grew sad. "I noticed during our journey through one of the villages of Elayas that we were not always welcome. They did not know I was their king, and they recognized that Johan was from another culture. Rather than showing hospitality to us, we were rejected for being different." His voice became firm. "We must pledge to work together to eliminate these attitudes born of ignorance and come together in unity and peace!"

Johan and Hamideh both leaned in, their eyes reflecting the light of the fire as they signaled their agreement, placing their hands over their hearts and bowing their heads briefly.

Rugal bowed in return, his eyes moist. He wiped them with the back of his hand before continuing. "Now, we face a common threat to all three of our peoples." He paused and looked to Hamideh. "It is my understanding that I will be facilitating your treaty with the Kargoliths to define what comprises their territory in three weeks. Is that correct?"

Hamideh smiled at Johan and nodded, "Yes, Rugal. We have a preliminary map of the territory that has already been approved by my father. When you return to mediate the treaty, it should merely be a formality."

Rugal, noting Johan nodding his head in approval, pumped his fist. "Excellent! It will be good to have our territories defined and leadership firmly in place." His expression turned serious. "We must not wait. The end of winter will be approaching, and we must be ready to stand together against the evil that will be assaulting our lands. We have much work to do to prepare."

With that somber reminder, the three young men looked at each other uncertainly. "When we started down this road to steal the Ring of Rosin," Johan began, "We never dreamed it would lead us here. But I am very glad it ended this way. My people also have a saying, *Three people are like a rope with three strands wrapped together. It is very hard to break.*" He looked at Rugal and Hamideh. "We are that rope."

Hamideh grinned. "A strong rope indeed."

"With many strengths," Rugal added. "Our destinies are intertwined. The Sepharim ceremony I want to conduct is simple but binds us together as brothers. We will need to lean into each other as brothers if we are to have any hope of defeating the coming evil. Are you with me?"

A resounding "Yes!" from both Johan and Hamideh rent the air, making Treble jump. The flutebird ruffled his feathers and then settled back onto his perch.

Rugal continued, "In participating, you join me in swearing to use your power only for good. That includes not only any *dynamis* you may possess, but the power entrusted to you by your people." Johan and Hamideh straightened and acknowledged Rugal's condition with firm nods, voicing their affirmation.

Rugal smiled warmly at the two young men across from him. "Let us begin the ceremony."

The flickering light from the fire danced across their faces. Rugal began the ancient ritual in the ancient language that started every Sepharim gathering, and Johan and Hamideh sat quietly, letting the unfamiliar words wash over them. Although they did not understand what Rugal was saying, they could sense the meaning and found his voice calming.

"Seidous man *dynamis* ferilux Elayas, Tolan, des Kargolith anthropoi shod." Rugal changed the last words of the traditional opening to include not only Elayas, but the kingdoms of Tolan and Kargolith. *We pledge our powers to defend the people of Elayas, Tolan, and Kargolith.*

Rugal gazed at Hamideh and Johan, meeting their eyes before he continued.

"The Sepharim is ever evolving to meet the needs of our people, while keeping our traditions that define who we are. I have sought and received permission from the Tamadar to induct you both into the Sepharim."

Hamideh gasped, "How is this possible? We are not citizens of Elayas!"

"After much discussion, it has been agreed that some things transcend citizenship," Rugal responded easily. "You are not giving up your allegiance to Tolan," he reassured the young man. "You are entering into a higher relationship, one that is concerned with every life, regardless of where they are born."

"But what...."

Before Johan could finish his objection, Rugal interrupted. "You have shown yourself worthy to be a member of the Sepharim not through the *dynamis* you do not possess, but because you reflect our highest values and your willingness to sacrifice your personal desires for the greater good. All you want is for your people to live peacefully and thrive, the same as Hamideh and me."

Rugal allowed Johan a moment before continuing. "Besides, I am not convinced that you yourself don't have *dynamis*, no matter how weak. Remember when you touched the arrow, and it became warm? The Ring of Rosin said that the arrow responds to *dynamis*. You may have a gift you are unaware of..." He paused and smiled. "But it doesn't matter. Either way, you are invited into the Sepharim if you so choose."

Rugal leaned forward, his gaze hopeful. "Will you each join me in the Sepharim and, in doing so, take the additional step of initiation?"

Johan and Hamideh looked at each other. Hamideh spoke up. "But...we are so different from each other. Look what happened to the two brothers in the Bird of the Mountains and the Stone of Fire fable. They were already brothers, but they argued and split apart. Can we overcome that?"

Rugal got to his feet and smiled. "We can't control the responses of others, but we can control our own." He looked at

Hamideh. "I choose you for my brother. Do you choose the Sepharim? Do you choose me?"

Hamideh stood up. "Yes!"

Rugal's gaze moved to Johan. "I choose you for my brother. Do you choose the Sepharim? Do you choose me?"

Johan jumped to his feet. "Yes!"

Rugal couldn't contain the grin on his face or the elation in his voice. "Then it is done. From this day forward, we are brothers for eternity."

He looked at his new brothers with pride and affection. "We don't know what the future brings, but we will face it together. I believe our differences will become our strengths." He gestured, and the three young men came together, grasping each other's arms in brotherly fashion. Rugal winked at his brothers and spoke with the authority of their newly forged bond, "Three people are like a rope with three strands wrapped together. It is very hard to break."

A brilliant flash of blue light engulfed them, filling them with warmth. Much to the young men's astonishment and joy, a green flash of light sprang from Hamideh, and a purple flash of light sprang from Johan, joining the blue. Seconds later, the lights disappeared. The ceremony was complete.

THE END OF BOOK TWO

THE CHARACTERS OF ELAYAS

Argothal: Dragon of the mountains; guardian of the Sword of Fate and the Ring of Rosin. Friend to King Rugal.

Bendar: Famous artist of Elayas.

Dendin: Young villager of Kepath.

Dungellan: Well-known warrior of the Kargoliths, and a member of the Mergolith tribe that merged with the Kargoliths.

Ethiod Stargazer: A master of the Sepharim and the most famous musician in Elayas.

Ethion: Ethiod's brother and innkeeper of the Stargazer Inn in Selba.

Evil Rider at River: A Neliph, member of the Neliphim Clan, their home is across the Argonean Sea.

Farin: Young page in King Rugal's court.

Felan: A master of the Sepharim who was Rugal's teacher until Felan was killed while defending an old man from one of Oldag's followers.

Flash: A big red horse that carries Rugal for part of his journey.

Gillian: Prince Hamideh's younger sister.

Hamideh: King Handerbin's son, who also is next in line to become king of Tolan.

Handerbin: King of Tolan, the country to the northwest of Elayas.

Jackal: Rugal's father. His real name is Aldon, and he is chosen by the Sepharim to help lead Rugal to his destiny.

Janar: A master of the Sepharim, he is Jackal's teacher and mentor.

Jardan: A shoemaker in Cargoa.

Johan of Sharvindar: An emissary from King Handerbin of Tolan, he remains a mystery. Johan goes by Jolan, when traveling in secret.

Kara: An original member of King Rosin's court, she is well-versed in court etiquette.

Kelar: Villager of Regos.

Krent: An evil minion of Oldag in Cargoa, known for his abuse of those weaker than he.

Legas: Member of the Sepharim and the Tamadar's contact in the village of Laran.

Lenar: A member of the Sepharim who serves as the Sepharim's representative in Farath.

Lissa: The daughter of Ethiod Stargazer, betrothed to Rugal.

Lona: Villager of Regos, an old woman who was a student at Selba before Oldag came to power.

Melad: Head steward of the castle where Rugal is king.

Mubarak: Leader in the village of Laran.

Mura: The wife of Jackal and the mother of Rugal, a strong and wise woman who has sacrificed much for her beliefs.

Nirkut: Member of the Sepharim and the Tamadar's contact in the village of Kepath.

Oldag: The evil usurper who betrayed King Rosin to gain the throne. Although his dark powers enabled him to keep his reign secure for many years, he was ultimately defeated by Rugal.

Philaten: Tamadar before the Swordsman, and his mentor.

Raksh: Johan of Sharvindar's horse, Raksh is dun-colored, compact, and sturdy.

Rohan: Member of the Kargoliths and Johan's younger brother.

Rosin: King before he was assassinated by Oldag, Rosin's rule was benevolent and prosperous.

Rugal: Reigning king of Elayas and Lissa's betrothed. Son of Jackal and Mura, he has the ability to change into more than one animal form. Rugal goes by Yandin when traveling in secret.

Silar: Villager of Laran and nephew of Mubarak.

Soldar: A member of Rosin's original court, he is well-versed in history and law.

The Swordsman: His given name is Zander. He holds the title of Tamadar, and is the leader of the Sepharim.

Tag: Rugal's favorite horse, he is a big, muscular bay.

Tonar: Rugal's friend and castle artist residing in Cargoa.

Treble: Flutebird who befriends Rugal.

Tuner: Flutebird who befriends Ethiod Stargazer.

Yandin: Young blacksmith apprentice from the village of Regos.

Zerdin: Cousin to Prince Hamideh of Tolan.

TERMINOLOGY OF ELAYAS

Bird of the Mountains: According to an ancient fable, upon finding the Stone of Fire, the Bird of the Mountains became its caretaker. Imbued with magical properties, including the ability to make music, the Bird of the Mountains was of tremendous size and magnificent beauty.

Day of Questioning: Occurring during the Year of Wisdom, once every ten years, this day has special significance because it is when the Time of Sun Shadow happens, enabling a rightful king, in possession of a ring made from the Stone of Fire, to ask questions. The ring will provide accurate answers to the king's questions, but only during the period of the Time of Sun Shadow.

Dynamis: A supernatural power (such as telepathic abilities or the ability to change to animal form) that is inherited. It is exhibited in different ways and is unique to each individual. Training by the Sepharim is important in order to be able to wield it most effectively.

Gormalins: Deadly creatures of evil that terrorized the citizens of Elayas and disappeared when Oldag was defeated.

Kargoliths: The nomadic tribe living in the unsettled territory between the kingdom of Tolan and the kingdom of Elayas.

Key of Power: Belonging to the rightful king of Elayas, it focuses and amplifies his *dynamis*, enabling it to be channeled for a long period of time without the usual fatigue that typically accompanies such effort.

Mergoliths: Two factions make up the Kargolith tribe. One faction is also called Kargoliths, and they comprise the majority of the tribe. The lesser faction, called the Mergoliths, came into the Kargolith tribe thirty years ago when their numbers were dwindling. While coming together with the Kargoliths, the Mergoliths have also retained their separate identity, which is a source of contention between the two factions.

Rite of Reciprocity: Available only during a new moon, a non-Kargolith can enter the sacred circle and request to be received as a native Kargolith. By doing so, they receive the same rights and privileges as a member of the tribe.

Sepharim: A group composed of both men and women, members follow a high code of ethics and have pledged to use their supernatural powers, known as *dynamis*, to protect the people of Elayas. Representatives of the Sepharim work closely with the king of Elayas and his court to maintain peace and forward positive initiatives in the kingdom.

Patriotes: Citizens of Elayas that do not possess *dynamis* but who were devoted to overthrowing Oldag and restoring the kingdom to the rightful heir, King Rugal. Patriotes worked with the Sepharim in returning their country to the same freedoms they enjoyed under King Rosin's reign.

Ring of Rosin: Commissioned by King Rosin, it is a red diamond set in a ring of gold. It glows and hums musically when worn by the true king.

Stone of Fire: Created when the foundations of the earth were laid, it is imbued with magical powers with the intention of aiding kingdoms in ruling peaceably. The stone has the ability to recognize the true ruler of a kingdom. Another magical property it possesses is the ability to impart knowledge to the true ruler during the Day of Questioning. No one knows the extent of its powers.

Sword of Fate: The sword of the king of Elayas, its bearer has the power to command the Sepharim when it is needed.

Tamadar: The leader of the Sepharim, his identity is kept secret so as to be more effective in serving his people.

Time of Sun Shadow: Occurring during the Day of Questioning, the Time of Sun Shadow is the time that the sun is completely engulfed in shadow, so that it is as if night has fallen.

Vellaquar: The name given to the Bird of the Mountains by the Kargoliths. Flutebirds are thought to have descended from the Bird of the Mountains, retaining the ability to make music found in her offspring.

Patrons: Chosen [illegible] that do not possess [illegible] Whosoever is [illegible] to overthrow the king and [illegible] the [illegible] to the [illegible] Royal Patrons [illegible] with [illegible] their [illegible] to the [illegible] they enjoyed under [illegible] Commission.

Ring of [illegible]: Commissioned by King [illegible] is a red diamond set [illegible] ring of gold [illegible] and [illegible] worthy [illegible].

[illegible] peaceably. The stone has the [illegible] to recognize the true ruler of [illegible] Another [illegible] [illegible] possesses [illegible] knowledge to the [illegible] one know [illegible]

Sword of [illegible]: The sword of the king of Ilyas [illegible] the power to command [illegible] people when it is [illegible].

[illegible]: the leader of the Sapbarin, his identity is kept secret so as to be more effective in serving his people.

Time of Sun Shadow: Occurring during the day of [illegible] the Time of Sun Shadow [illegible] the sun is [illegible] completely engulfed in shadow, so that it is as if night has fallen.

Velladine: The [illegible] given to the [illegible] of the [illegible] Mountains by the [illegible] Queen [illegible] known to have descended from the [illegible] of the Mountains, retaining the ability to [illegible] the [illegible] and [illegible] spring.

Kargolith Tribal Ancestry

Ancient Fable

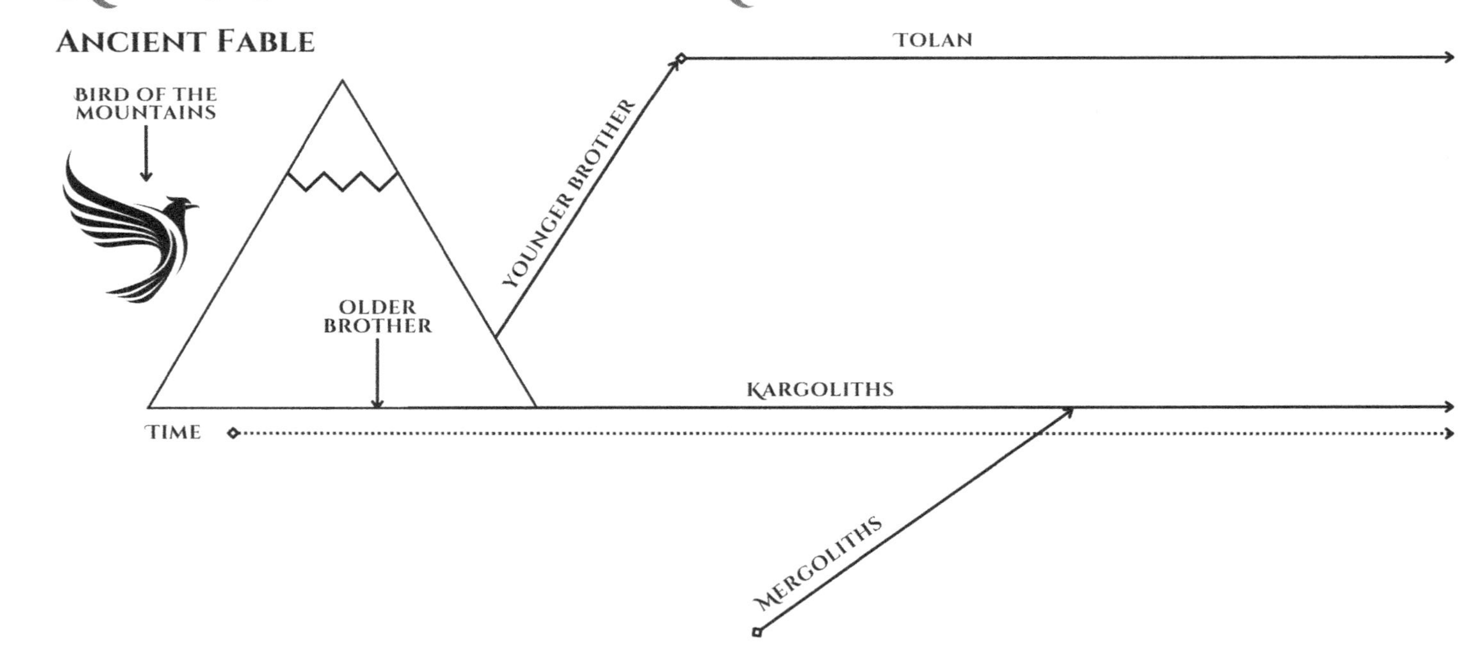

Ancient Tolan Legend on Scroll

In an age of yore, in times long gone,
When magic thrived, and legends shone,
A wondrous bird took flight alone,
Toward the peaks of mountains' throne.
In its talons, gripped so tight,
A mighty stone of blazing light.
A quest it bore through day and night,
To lay it down where shadows fright.
Yet, ere the bird could reach its goal,
The stone slipped free, beyond control.
It shattered 'pon the earth beneath,
Each shard aglow, a fire did seep.
"This Rock of Fire, my charge to keep,"
The bird did wail, and then did weep.
"For if these fragments men complete,
A power vast, they then shall reap."
But power calls to hearts of men,
With pride and greed, again, again.
Beware the fire, the perilous boon,

Lest shadows fall 'neath blood-red moon.
So heed this tale of ancient lore,
Of fiery rocks and quests of yore.
For those who seek, and fragments store,
Beware strength unknown lies at your door.

THE FABLE OF THE BIRD OF THE MOUNTAINS AND THE STONE OF FIRE

The mountains stood for none but brave,
With beauty rugged, wild to save.
Some were drawn, while others turned,
The rarest birds with power earned.
One bird was called, the keeper grand,
Of the stone of fire, in mountain's hand.
Two brothers bold, with hearts so free,
Left their home for destiny.
The peak they sought, from village far,
To find the bird, and steal its star.
For the stone held magic rare,
Its power they'd seize with daring flair.
When manhood came to the younger's side,
Plans were laid with careful pride.
Supplies they took, farewells they bade,
Upon their horses, a journey made.
Into the range, their path they chose,
Majestic peak, where adventure rose.
At its base, they camped in sight,

Prepared to climb at morning light.
The sun arose, the day begun,
Quick they ate, the climb was won.
Horses hobbled, packs were packed,
Upward they went, the goal exact.
The air was cool, their water drank,
Following wise men's advice, they sank.
Tiny dots, their horses below,
The lake a puddle, their spirits aglow.
In silence climbed, with focused care,
Slipping not on terrain so bare.
A crevasse they saw, the bird's own home,
Excitement shared, they'd soon atone.
A precipice blocked their sought way,
Younger would climb, without delay.
Up he went, with nimble might,
When the bird emerged, in furious flight.
With claws of fire, the stone it bore,
The older brother's choice was sore.
To save his kin or seize the stone,
He tried for both, in frantic tone.
The stone dislodged, and shards did fall,
Saving his brother, the elder gave his all.
The bird's shriek echoed, pain and rage,
Younger rolled, with scarred visage.
Though life was saved, anger grew,
The brothers fought; their bond askew.
Back at camp, they parted ways,
the younger northward went, in newfound days.
The younger found a home anew,
In Tolan's land, his life pursued.
Married, settled, a kingdom grown,
Tolan's founder, his legacy shown.

The older stayed, his wisdom known,
As tribal leader, he had grown.
When crops did fail, his guidance clear,
In nomadic life, he quelled their fears.
They roamed the lands, with wisdom's gifts,
And took the name of Kargoliths.
In the ancient tongue, they're known,
As travelers, where winds have blown.
Singular or many, the name implies,
Kargoliths exist, beneath open skies.

KEY OF POWER

A DYNAMIS NOVEL - BOOK THREE

He is evil beyond comprehension and possesses magic through his arrows. He and his people live across the sea. He will return and bring companions with the intent to destroy all of you. Your futures are dependent on your kingdoms working together. You, Johan, and Hamideh are marked, and each of you will have to give up something you hold dear for the greater good. Even so, there are no assurances. The future is cloudy.

The Ring of Rosin has revealed the evil rider with his deadly arrows is returning with a vengeance...will King Rugal and his allies be able to defend their kingdoms, or will they be destroyed by the dark magic wielded by the coming threat from across the sea?

The adventure awaits... 2025

ACKNOWLEDGMENTS

Writing a book is not an easy endeavor; it takes discipline and sacrifice. While much joy is found in storytelling and putting one's creativity on paper to share with the world, it also requires long hours at the keyboard, often putting other activities and time with family on hold. Knowing that the end result is an entertaining story that perhaps will find its way into the hearts of my readers keeps me motivated, but the task is still huge and would not be possible to accomplish without the help of many people.

My husband Phil never ceases to amaze me with how he takes care of our household so I can focus on writing. He is an incredible partner in all things, and I am so grateful we are on this adventure called life together. Phil is very talented and is an invaluable collaborator in my brainstorming process. He has a unique perspective that has enriched the telling of my tales, and he is my favorite beta reader. Much of what you read has his stamp on it.

Having the support of our son Joshua and daughter-in-love Naomi is truly a blessing. They not only encourage me and uplift me, celebrating my author milestones and praying for me–they also offer tangible help in the areas of their gifting. Josh is always available for a quick consult on word choice and joined me a second time to work on the map together–which has been updated to reflect the events of the story. Naomi is a very talented artist. I have leveraged her expertise and creativity countless times during the creation of the graphics associated with Ring of Rosin.

I had a vision for the cover of Ring of Rosin, and I am very grateful to Piere D'arterie for bringing it to such vibrant life. He has been very patient with my many requests, and I am thrilled with his creation, which showcases my story with his stunning visual elements.

I am so grateful to Joseph Fredrickson for his editing expertise. He is a true wordsmith and a joy to work with. Joey's passion for not only editing but exploring the meaning of words and how they impact the story, invigorates my writing while making the process fun. Joseph is also responsible for the poetic renditions of the fable found on the scroll and relayed in more detail to Rugal during Johan's telling—a beautiful addition to Ring of Rosin for all of us to enjoy!

Beta readers are such an important part of the writing process. Their feedback informs the author of what works well and what doesn't, points out plot holes, comments on character development, what areas may need more work, and is a treatise for understanding if the book is being received as the author intends. A special thank you to my beta readers for Ring of Rosin. My wonderful husband, Phil Golden, pointed out some mechanical details that needed to be changed to prevent you, dear reader, from being jarred out of the story. He has a special talent for that.

My amazing granddaughter, Rose Randall, kept me motivated to write Ring of Rosin. She was not happy after reading Sword of Fate and then finding out that the next book in the series wasn't ready. Not wanting to make her and all my readers wait too long, I got to work. I also recruited Rose as a beta reader. My granddaughter is very happy the next book in the series is finished, and she did a great job providing feedback – Ring of Rosin is *Granddaughter Approved*! Win-win! Now, she is waiting for Key of Power...

It is also important to get the eyes of professionals on my books for their feedback before releasing it to the world. For Ring of Rosin, I utilized the platform Fiverr to find talented freelancers with experience in beta reading. Special thanks to Stella Marvin and Stephen B. for lending their expertise to the project.

So many people in my life continue to contribute to my writing through their love and encouragement. Writing a book (especially fiction) is very challenging. Keeping track of all of the pieces while weaving an exciting tale that will entertain and uplift readers can be a daunting task. I am very grateful for those who cheer me on, providing the emotional support that helps me find joy in my labor, even when it's hard.

Jane Vaughan, Eddie and Susan Venetucci, Katherine Evanson, Mary Oller, Andrea Amosson, Ross Irvin, Ashley Skoczynski, Stephanie Newland, and so many others have contributed to my literary efforts with their support, love, and encouragement. My stories reflect the importance of relationships in our lives, and I treasure each one.

Last year my amazing husband took me on a ranch vacation so that I could experience my "bucket list" item of getting to work cattle. Cutting calves out of a herd is one of the most exhilarating things I have ever done. Phil and I got to meet some wonderful people during our stay. Jeff Kuschner and Ralph Brandofino quickly became friends, and they were so encouraging and supportive when they found out I am an author. The easy camaraderie that developed was a precious gift we all enjoyed, whether riding horses, sharing a meal, or sitting on a front porch chatting into the night. We may not have solved all of the world's problems, but we did figure out the best way to end a conversation - *with a hug!* Thanks to Jeff and Ralph for your friendship across our shared love of horses. I will always treasure the memories we made at Sylvan Dale.

A special thanks to Steven and Kimberly Deans and their Princess Gillian. There is something very precious about old friends, and when they are excited about my books, well, it makes it extra sweet. Gillian never fails to inspire all of us, and I am looking forward to her role in Key of Power.

A few days ago, I was sitting in front of my computer and found myself teary-eyed. I am most grateful of all for my Lord and Savior, Jesus Christ, and I feel incredibly humbled that God has blessed me with the ability to write books. To be able to sit at a keyboard and have a story pour out is a very special gift. I pray God uses it to bless many and that the work of my hands is always a "Light in the Darkness" for His glory.

About the Author

Nancy Golden wears a lot of different hats – She is a wife and mom, author, engineer, professor, horsewoman, and small business owner. She is a follower of Jesus Christ. She is a member of the National Space Society and also the founder of a writing group – the Carrollton League of Writers.

Nancy lives in a suburb of Dallas, Texas and loves to ride bicycles and horses. She has been a Trekkie for as long as she can remember and always wanted to ride a dragon.

Catch up on Nancy's latest writing endeavors and other fun stuff at nancygoldenbooks.com

I had a lot of fun writing both Sword of Fate and Ring of Rosin, and I am very excited to share them with you. If you haven't read Sword of Fate yet, it is Book One in the *Dynamis* series, and I suggest you do. Sword of Fate will provide some great backstories for many of the characters you met in Ring of Rosin.

I hope you enjoy reading both books! If you do, please recommend them to your family and friends. Teachers may also want to consider them for their classroom libraries and can visit my website to download a free curriculum guide for Sword of Fate.

Being an author is hard work, but it is also a joy. My heart's desire is for the words I write to have a positive impact on my readers and brighten their day–that is my wish for you. You can email me directly at nancy@goldencrossranch.com with any comments. I would love to hear from you!

One of the best things you can do for any author is leave a review–I hope you'll consider doing so.

Also by Nancy Golden

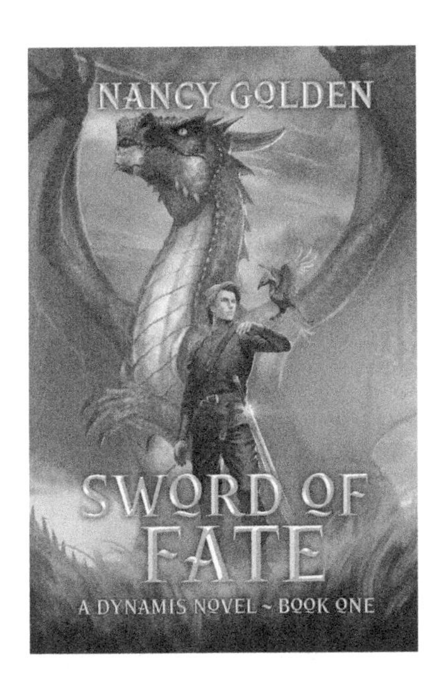

ALIEN
NEIGHBORS
NANCY GOLDEN

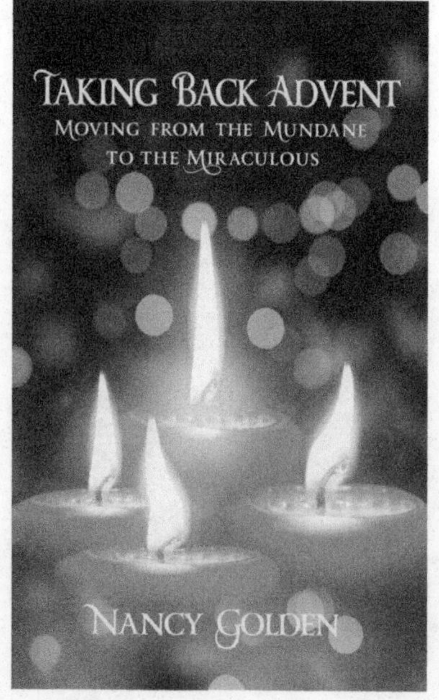
TAKING BACK ADVENT
MOVING FROM THE MUNDANE
TO THE MIRACULOUS
NANCY GOLDEN

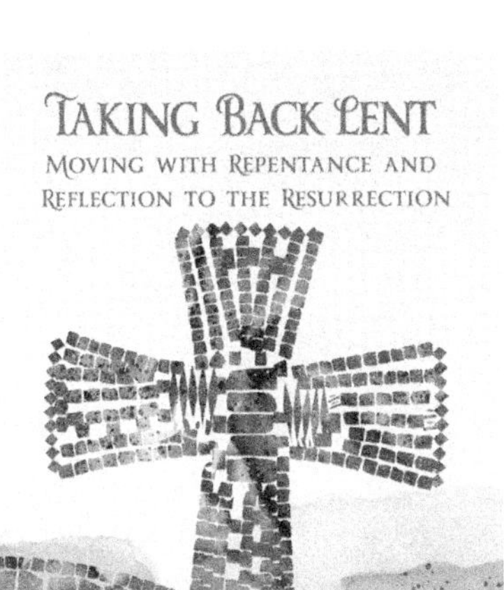
TAKING BACK LENT
MOVING WITH REPENTANCE AND
REFLECTION TO THE RESURRECTION
NANCY GOLDEN